AF416511

A DADDY FOR HANNA:

A DDLG ROMANCE

SUE LYNDON

A Daddy for Hanna: A DDlg Romance
Copyright © 2022 by Sue Lyndon

All rights reserved

No part of this document may be reproduced or transmitted in any form or by any means, electronic, mechanical, photocopying, recording, or otherwise, without prior written permission of Sue Lyndon. All names, brands, characters, and settings are purely from the author's imagination, and any resemblance to real people, real brands, and real locations is a coincidence. Contact: suelyndon@suelyndon.com

Editing by Celeste Jones

Cover design by Angela Haddon Book Cover Design

Published in the United States of America
Sue Lyndon
www.suelyndon.com

CHAPTER 1

HANNA HELD UP A SMALL, faded mirror to inspect her appearance. A pair of haunted but determined blue eyes stared back. A hint of golden hair peeked from beneath her black kapp, and her cheeks looked paler than usual, almost sickly.

Apprehension twisted her stomach, but her pulse raced with determination.

She placed the mirror down and glanced around her small room, making certain all the belongings she wished to take had already been gathered.

A quick getaway was necessary. A bag containing her few treasures waited between two rocks in the cornfield. She'd placed it there two days prior.

The aroma of baking bread and the light clatter of dishes greeted her as she tiptoed down the steps, careful not to wake her youngest nieces and nephews who were still asleep. Her sister-in-law, Sarah, was always the first one awake. Normally Hanna would take a place beside her to get breakfast started. Today wasn't a normal day though.

She paused at the bottom of the steps and closed her eyes, imagining what her life would be like if she stayed. Emptiness consumed her, giving her the resolve to keep moving and not back down from the difficult decision she'd already made.

The expectations that rested on her shoulders were a burden she refused to bear. The life she faced if she stayed in his house, and in this community, was a blackness enveloping her soul and her very will to live.

Change was the only cure.

The only way to change was to leave.

She'd known this her whole life, even as a small child.

She approached the kitchen and lingered in the doorway. "Sarah?"

"Good morning, Hanna. Help me with these pie crusts. The babies will be awake soon. I have eggs and oatmeal ready." Sarah glanced over her shoulder, a fatigued but content look on her face. She truly belonged here. She fit in and Hanna doubted she'd ever questioned her place here.

"I'm leaving, Sarah."

"What?" Sarah turned to give her a sharp, disapproving scowl.

"I'm not going to join the church. I'm certain of it, and now I know I must leave."

"Where will you go?"

Hanna debated telling Sarah of her plan but quickly decided against it. No one would follow her or try to bring her back, but it still seemed best to keep it a secret. "I'll be fine. Trust me. I have a place to go and know someone who will help me find Eli."

The color drained from Sarah's face. "How dare you speak his name?" She turned to focus on the pie crust, dusting it with flour before rolling it out with angry movements.

Until now, Hanna had only whispered her oldest brother, Eli's, name in secret, tucked under her covers at night. Even when she visited the English neighbor, Ben Foster, who allowed her to send Eli letters from his address, she'd never uttered his name as loud as she had just now.

It felt right. Liberating.

Hanna's gaze traveled around the plain house. The walls threatened to close in. It was a heavy feeling that never left her, a suffocating tightness in her chest that sometimes clouded her vision, one that had started not long after her mother's passing when Hanna was but five years old.

The truth was, nothing about being Amish felt right.

Deep down, she'd always known she hadn't belonged. Not really.

She'd always felt like an outsider among her own people.

The few interactions she'd had with the English energized her and made her long for a different life. A life far away from these Pennsylvania mountains.

Eli lived in Oregon, and she hoped beyond hope to see his face again.

Hanna straightened and stared at her sister-in-law's back. "Good-bye, Sarah. I told the babies good-bye last night when I tucked them in."

Sarah continued rolling out the dough with her back to Hanna. At least she had tried to leave on good terms, though there was really no such thing. Not in this family.

Joining the church was supposed to be a highly personal decision, one that others in her community were meant to respect. But her father didn't see it that way. If she didn't join the church, she would be considered dead to him. Even worse than dead. Erased from existence. He would act as though she'd been forever banished for committing some terrible sin, and Sarah would live the rest of her life never speaking Hanna's name, as would the rest of the family.

The very thought of it broke her heart, and yet she still couldn't stay.

Hanna wondered if any of her family members would whisper her name in secret while tucked under their covers at night like she did for her brother Eli.

The solitude she felt within her huge Amish community had always been her secret sorrow. She'd tried so hard to capture the sense of community her family and friends felt here, the genuine happiness she saw all around her, but it was no use.

After years of trying to force it, she'd finally realized it couldn't be forced.

The screen door banged shut as she fled the house. The early August air was cool but promised a warm day. From the front porch, she scanned the farm through the dim morning light.

To her left over the tree-covered mountain, the horizon glowed pink with the imminence of sunrise. At this early hour, the best place to find her daat was in the barn.

Determined to face him bravely, she took a deep breath and set off.

Nerves turned her stomach sour, her heart accelerated, and her palms broke into a sweat.

Was this how Eli had felt before his departure? Brave yet terrified at the same time?

"Daat?" She crept through the open doors. The smell of hay and animals surrounded her. Two kittens scampered across the floor and into the shadows. "Daat?"

"I'm here, Hanna." From behind an out-of-order milking machine, he popped up and wiped his brow on the back of his sleeve. He scratched at his thick, brown beard and raised an eyebrow. "What is it? Why are you wearing shoes?"

She glanced at her feet. During the summer, the only reason she, as well as Sarah and the children, had to wear shoes outside was to go to church or for a rare trip into town. In contrast, her daat and brothers worked around machinery and large animals, so they wore boots year-round.

She finally met her father's gaze, his impatient scrutiny, and she suppressed a shudder.

"I've made a decision about joining the church," she said.

The large vein on his temple pulsed. Anger, a warning, flared in his cold blue eyes. He swallowed hard and wiped at his brow again. "And?"

"I've decided not to. I'm here to say good-bye."

"You're a foolish girl!" he spat out, rounding the milking machine to approach her. Though he walked with a limp, she instinctively backed up, ready to make a fast escape should he become violent. "The Devil's Playground looks good to you, does it?"

Hanna trembled and stepped back. "This life isn't for me, and I wish you would respect that as you ought to. I feel I must point out that others who leave our community are still welcomed by their families for visits." She gestured to the door behind her, looking at the rolling fields behind the house. "I don't belong. Just like Eli didn't belong. I can't stay for one more day."

"Do not speak his name! You're forsaking your family and friends. Not to mention God and His plan for you. If you leave, you'll have no one. Nothing." He paused and softened his voice. "You're part of this family. You can't leave. We care about you."

Her throat burned, but she'd resolved not to allow his words to sway her, no matter what he said. In her heart, she believed her daat cared more about his reputation in the community and how a second child leaving would affect his image. First Eli. Now her. He would probably say or do anything to make her stay.

A noise caught her attention, and she spotted a few of her younger cousins, who lived on a nearby farm and frequently visited to help in the mornings, peering at them from behind a ladder that led up to the loft. The sight of their little faces almost broke her resolve. Oh how she would miss them, and her arms ached to hug them one last time.

"Go tend to the goats!" her daat growled, his face reddening more by the second. Her cousins scrambled away, and Hanna hated that she wouldn't be able to say good-bye to them all. Daat would prevent her from speaking to anyone else before she left—of that she had no doubt.

"I'm leaving now," she said, angry with herself for trying to say her farewells. What had she expected? A hug and well wishes? An invitation to visit the farm whenever she liked? Not likely.

His bushy eyebrows pinched together and he limped forward. He held a wrench in his hand, and the livid expression he wore revealed his intentions. Her stomach flipped, and she turned and ran from the barn without a backward glance. She had no wish to see his anger or to feel it. Those days had come to an end.

As she passed the woodshop where her brothers, Jacob and Abram, spent their mornings, she paused to gaze through the windows. She spotted them moving about the shop but shrank away from an encounter with them. After being shut out by Sarah and her own daat, she couldn't bear the thought of another cold rejection.

No one called out her name, and no one came running after her as she headed for the cornfield. It took a few minutes to reach the rocks where she'd hidden her bag. Luckily it hadn't rained. She peeked inside, inspecting the contents. A hairbrush, a skein of her favorite yarn, several crochet hooks, a small sewing kit, a pen, a set of correspondence cards, her birth certificate, an apron, and two dark blue dresses identical to the one she had on. No food. No water. No money. Nothing of any real value. Yet Hanna wasn't worried. Not much, anyway.

She had a plan.

As she exited the field and made for the forest path she knew well, the rising sun chased the shadows out of the tall trees and underbrush. Hanna walked slowly, keeping her attention on the narrow trail. A blacksnake had bitten her in the forest last year while she was picking berries, and she had no desire to repeat that painful experience, even though none of the local snakes were venomous. Eli had taught her all about snakes and bears and bobcats—the only real threat posed by nature near the farm. The best way to keep safe when alone was to make noise, so she hummed the tune to "In the Still Isolation," her favorite childhood song.

The path ahead led to the Hartzlers' farm, but Hanna didn't intend to stop there. If she stayed in the woods and traveled a bit farther, she would happen upon Ben Foster's property. Mr. Foster lived in the middle of the forest and rarely left his home. He was kind and trustworthy though, and he had helped Eli when he'd left home years ago.

She smiled as she recalled the one and only letter Eli had sent to the farm. She'd intercepted it and tossed it into the fire before her daat could find it. It had been a simple note addressed to her. Eli had been brief and vague, only telling her that he'd spent time living with and working for Mr. Foster, but that he'd eventually traveled across the country and met a nice woman in Oregon, where he planned to settle down. He'd assured her Mr. Foster was a decent man she could trust, and she would be able to visit his home and write Eli letters without their daat finding out. And so, she'd been sneaking away to Mr. Foster's cabin for the last three years.

The forest grew thicker, and Hanna recognized her surroundings enough to know she was halfway there. Only two more miles to go. Mr. Foster claimed it was a four-mile walk to his house from her farm.

Her insides softened as her anticipation over seeing Mr. Foster grew. She hadn't stopped by in a few weeks, and she'd missed seeing him something fierce.

The last time she'd visited him, she'd come upon

him shirtless while he was chopping wood, though he'd quickly donned a t-shirt once he'd noticed her standing there staring at him. At the time, she'd been shocked by his nudity, but also mesmerized by his gleaming chest and sculpted muscles, not to mention his powerful biceps which had flexed impressively as he'd lifted the axe before bringing it down to split the wood.

She waved a hand in front of her face, suddenly hot and needing to fan herself.

It struck her as strange as she continued, ducking under branches and brushing away cobwebs, that she was thinking so hard about Mr. Foster, imagining the smile he would greet her with, and wondering whether or not he would be clean-shaven or showing a few days of dark stubble.

Shouldn't she be despairing over never seeing her family again? She blinked a few times, testing her eyes as she thought of never seeing her daat again.

Nothing. No burning sensation in her eyes or her throat.

Vaguely, she wondered if she could learn to cry again. She hadn't cried since she was a small child and her father had broken her of the habit. He hadn't permitted crying, not even when someone died, like her mother. Not even when the brother you cared for most left for good. She'd wanted to cry an ocean of tears for Eli, but she'd had to swallow her grief and pretend nothing had happened.

"Eli," she said, lifting her chin to the trees. "Eli, Eli, Eli!" She shouted his name at the sky.

As she came into a small clearing in the woods, she stopped to gather her thoughts.

The memories of her first visit to Mr. Foster's home rushed back. He'd been expecting her, and he'd gone out of his way to make her feel welcome and comfortable that first time. She'd never met him, never known about him until reading Eli's letter. Had she known Eli was only a few miles away, she would've run off to visit him as much as possible.

Mr. Foster, however, had helped her understand Eli's reasons for keeping silent for years—her brother had thought her too young to safely sneak away, and he'd worried about the ramifications if their daat ever found out.

Hanna took a few more steps and eyed the cabin with a wraparound porch. Ben Foster's residence. Would he assist her in her quest for independence, just as he'd helped her brother years before?

Only one way to find out.

She smoothed her hands over her skirt and stepped into the clearing.

CHAPTER 2

L‌ADY JUMPED from her spot on the rug and bounded to the front door to bark at nothing. Or maybe it was something. Ben rubbed his eyes and traipsed out of the kitchen, wondering if a herd of deer were passing by. Whatever Lady was making a fuss about, it likely wasn't another man. Ben didn't even have a real driveway leading to the main road a few miles away. Just a dirt path, covered with grass and weeds, with a mailbox situated along the road. He doubted anyone in their right mind would venture on this path that wound through the trees to his cabin. Exactly the reason he'd built on this land.

Guaranteed privacy.

"Calm down, Lady. You've had your breakfast. You don't need to go chasing after any deer." He stroked his trusted dog's head. Her barking ceased, replaced by a whimper as she sat impatiently, her tail wagging.

All the thick curtains were drawn, and the small glass pane in the front door didn't reveal anything nearby. Ben moved to the living room window to pull the fabric aside.

"Oh, damn," he muttered when a small Amish girl appeared on the edge of the forest. He watched as she stopped and stared at his cabin. A small bag hung over her shoulder. When she finally began to walk again, Ben looked down at Lady. "It's only Hanna. Why don't you go say hello?"

Ben slid aside the two metal deadbolts, unlocked the knob, and flung the door wide open for Lady. The energetic German Shepherd barreled outside. Ben couldn't help smiling. While Hanna's visits made him uneasy, he'd also found himself anticipating them more and more.

When a few weeks passed without her dropping by, he spent way too much time glancing out the windows, wondering when she would appear in the clearing. She tended to visit in the afternoons, and for this reason she never failed to pass through his thoughts each day after lunch.

The heat of the day hit him hard as he jogged down the porch steps. Hanna was crouched on the ground, rubbing Lady's stomach while the dog licked her face. Lady would've ripped anyone else's throat out who stepped foot on his property, except for Hanna. Well, Eli too. But he was long gone and sent letters in his stead.

"Good morning, Mr. Foster!" Hanna giggled as Lady continued her silly antics.

"Good morning, Hanna." He eyed the bag she'd dropped beside her. What the hell was in there?

"I'm afraid I don't have any new letters from Eli. He's probably waiting until Annabel has the baby so he can write with good news. But if you'd like to come in and write him a new letter, you're more than welcome."

The sadness in her expression when she glanced up tugged at his heart. Something was wrong. Seriously wrong. He ached to rush forward and gather her up, bring her inside, and hold her while she told him of all her troubles. He cared for the sweet young woman, and hoped she wasn't as miserable as Eli had been on the farm. He knew her father was a difficult man who expected near perfection from all those who lived under his roof.

"Come on, Lady, leave the poor girl alone. It's not like I don't give you enough attention." At his command, the dog raced onto the porch, her tail still wagging and her big pink tongue hanging from her mouth.

Hanna grabbed her bag and rose to her feet. When her gaze flickered over him, the sadness in her eyes transformed to uncertainty. He had the distinct feeling she was about to ask for something.

Help.

Could it be true? His heart raced. Was she following in Eli's footsteps and leaving her family behind? Dare he hope?

He winced. His reasons for wanting her to leave her family were dark indeed.

Fantasies involving her writhing underneath him during the throes of passion visited him on sleepless nights. Sometimes during the days too.

Despite his fantasies though, he simply wanted her to be happy and healthy, whether she was tucked in her bed on the farm or... elsewhere.

"Come on inside, Hanna. It's only going to get hotter today. I'll get you a cold drink."

"Thank you, Mr. Foster." She breezed past him, her dark blue dress grazing his leg as he held the door open.

Excitement surged through him at the close contact, and he tried to tamp it down. As he turned to face her, he glimpsed an errant strand of golden hair poking out of her black kapp, running down the side of her neck. That, along with the vision of her flushed face and pretty blue eyes, nearly caused him to come undone.

She was too pretty.

Too young and ripe and, most of all, tempting.

It was official. Ben Foster had a one-way ticket to hell.

Christ, she was young enough to be his daughter.

"Come have a seat at the table." Careful not to touch her, he guided her to the kitchen and pulled out a chair. Head bowed as more pink stained her cheeks, she placed her bag on the floor next to the chair, sat down slowly, and folded her hands in her lap.

Ben busied himself by pouring two glasses of iced tea. A million questions buzzed through his mind. Certainly Hanna wasn't here to check her correspondence with Eli. Though she was generally on the shy side, her demeanor was off balance today. Besides that, she'd never visited him in the morning before.

He delivered her drink and sat across from her. An awkward silence stretched between them as they sipped the tea. Her face remained flushed so prettily, and another strand of hair had fallen from her kapp. With each breath she took, her chest heaved up and down, drawing his gaze to her breasts, which were unfortunately well-hidden underneath the plain dress. In his imagination though, he pictured her firm, pale mounds, and hardened, dark pink nipples clearly.

He shook away the image and placed his glass down, leaning forward to peer directly in her eyes. "What's happened, Hanna? Are you all right?" He surveyed her face for bruises, knowing her father had a heavy hand, or at least he had with Eli. To his relief, he saw no hint of bruises, fresh or fading.

She blinked a few times and set her drink down. "I-I'll be nineteen next month."

Nineteen. Christ Almighty. Young, innocent, and Amish. Yep, not only did Ben have a one-way ticket to hell, but he had a seat reserved in the first-class section.

"Is that a problem?" he asked, trying to ignore the stirring in his loins. "You turning nineteen? You getting married soon or something?" Jealousy rippled through him at the possibility.

She inhaled deeply and smiled when Lady curled up at her feet under the table.

"My daat thinks I should have joined the church already. He's been asking me almost every day about it."

"You left." He regarded her with wonder and respect. Most girls who didn't want to join the Amish church would've done so anyway. None of them had much of a choice. It was a matter of survival. With no education beyond the eighth grade and no immediate job opportunities, leaving was a near impossibility. Yet Hanna had done just that.

"I did," she finally said, reaching down to scratch Lady's ear. "I told my daat I'd decided not to join the church." She shrugged. "It happened this morning and I know I'm already dead to him. Sarah even refused to say good-bye to me. She turned her back and refused to look at me, and she's the most open-minded of them all. I didn't bother telling Abram and Jacob good-bye. I knew they would treat me the same as Daat and Sarah. It makes me very sad. In other Amish families, the children who don't join the church are not written off as outcasts. Their decision is respected, and they are still usually able to visit with their families. But my father..." Her voice trailed off and she pressed her lips tightly together.

"Eli came to me like this one day," Ben said. The memory of a sixteen-year-old Amish boy came rushing back. Eli had shown up on his porch with a black eye and a swollen jaw, asking if Ben had any work for him. Against his better judgment, Ben offered Eli some work and a place to stay. It was supposed to be temporary, but he'd stayed for two years. The longer he stayed, the more Ben wanted to help him. After Eli earned his G.E.D., he'd left with the wages he'd painstakingly saved to find his place in the world, a young man of eighteen years. He'd done well for himself, too, and Ben was incredibly proud of him.

"Mr. Foster?" Hanna gnawed at her lower lip. "You're the only friend I have. I-I was hoping you could help me the way you helped Eli. I'm not asking for charity, but I'd ask you to help me find work. I'm a hard worker. I can do most anything."

Ben studied her, taken aback. He had hoped she would directly ask to work for him, the way Eli had worked for him, doing chores and laboring around the cabin while Ben worked to build a series of underground storage rooms that connected to the basement, back when Ben was going through a survivalist phase.

"Hanna, I feel uncomfortable helping you find work."

Her face fell. "Oh." Her chair scratched the floor as she stood up. Her hands trembled, and she clasped them together as her gaze ventured near him, though she didn't quite meet his eyes. "I will leave you, then. I'm sorry to take up your time. Thank you for the tea."

"Wait. Sit back down, Hanna. I wasn't finished speaking."

Slowly, she returned to her seat, sitting down with her back stiff. Lady rose to place her head in

Hanna's lap. The dog whimpered and stared up at her with compassionate, large black eyes.

"I can't in good conscience send you out into the world cold turkey. It's a scary place out there for someone like you. People might take advantage of you, and I'd hate to see any harm come to you. Eli became like a son to me, and I would never turn his sister out. Besides, Hanna, I consider you a friend too. I can find some work for you around the cabin. I can even help you earn your G.E.D." He leaned back in his chair, his decision made. "You're staying here, Hanna. That's final."

CHAPTER 3

WIND CHIMES CLATTERED FAINTLY as the scent of baking bread filled the house. Hanna wiped her hands on her apron and inspected the kitchen. The floor could use a good mopping and the counters a good scrubbing. Even the walls needed to be wiped down. It pleased her to find yet another chore to occupy her time, and her mind.

As she gathered the necessary supplies from a closet in the hallway, her thoughts drifted to Mr. Foster.

Living with a man the way she was right now was downright sinful, yet she didn't feel like she was behaving badly. Knowing he considered her a friend brought a smile to her lips. She liked him more than she'd liked most Amish.

That thought caused her smile to fade.

As much as she tried not to think of her daat, her brothers, Sarah, her cousins, and her little nieces and nephews, they sometimes crept into her thoughts. Even though they were only a few miles apart, she doubted she would ever see them again, unless it happened by accident. Even then, they wouldn't speak to her, let alone look at her. Not unless she returned to the farm and decided to join the church.

Not likely.

A week had passed since she'd arrived at Mr. Foster's house. Since then, he'd handed all the cooking and cleaning duties over to her.

Not that it was a lot of work...

She suspected he was indulging her and trying to find work just to make her feel happy and needed. He spent most of his time in the greenhouse out back, in a workroom next to his bedroom that contained several computers, and fishing in a nearby stream.

She also had the distinct impression he was trying to avoid her as much as possible, but she couldn't put her finger on why. He was nothing but kind to her, but she frequently sensed his unease in her presence.

Likewise, she felt uneasy around him, especially in the evenings when he came inside for the night. The cabin seemed much smaller then.

"Smells good."

Hanna started and gasped, spinning around to meet Mr. Foster face-to-face. "You scared me!" she said, half scolding. As she fought to catch her breath, they both burst into laughter. It was the first time she'd seen him laugh since her arrival. It brought her hope.

Maybe the tension between them only existed in her head.

"I'm sorry, Hanna. I didn't mean to startle you."

She flashed him a smile. "It's all right, Mr. Foster. Lunch isn't quite ready yet. Can I fix you a snack?"

"No, I'm fine. I wanted to talk to you about something."

Her stomach flipped at the sudden seriousness of his expression. "What is it?"

"You're still wearing your Amish clothes, even the kapp," he said, pointing at her head. "I took Eli clothes shopping not long after he came to stay with me. I'd like to do the same for you."

Dumbfounded, Hanna stared at him. Was it right to accept his offer? Deep in the woods in his secluded cabin, they were alone, and while she wasn't Amish anymore, she hadn't thought of changing her appearance yet. Instead, finding work had been her top priority. Now that she had work and a safe place to stay, she supposed it was time to change the way she looked.

"Thank you. That sounds nice, but please deduct the cost of clothing from my wages." She didn't want to be a burden. Mr. Foster had agreed to pay her monthly, a generous sum she'd argued was too much, and he'd even promised to help her set up her own checking account soon. The idea of a trip into town to experience this rite of passage into the English world filled her with excitement.

Mr. Foster sighed and smiled faintly. "All right. If you insist. We'll go to town tomorrow morning, visit the mall, and go to a restaurant for lunch."

The mall. Lunch in a real restaurant. Hanna couldn't believe it. She beamed at Mr. Foster. "Thank you."

His smile disappeared and he regarded her with a thoughtful look. "Here. I want to try something." His deep voice rumbled through her insides, making her feel shaky and unsettled and... achy between her thighs. Her face flushed. She didn't understand the visceral reactions she kept having to Mr. Foster's nearness and his deep voice.

Before she realized his intentions, he reached out to touch her kapp. She forgot how to breathe as he tried pulling it off. It didn't budge. She restrained a nervous laugh.

"Mr. Foster, it's pinned on tight. Would you like me to remove it?"

"Yes, Hanna." He gulped, and a strange look entered his eyes. Excitement? "I want to see you," he said.

The intensity of his gaze called to her heart and caused her hands to shake.

Why couldn't she breathe? And why was her heart racing so?

Ignoring the trembling of her fingers, she took the pins out of the kapp, one by one, laying them on the countertop. Once the kapp was free, she pulled it off and sat it next to the pins. She stole a glance at Mr. Foster. He appeared confused, probably because her hair hadn't fallen down about her shoulders after losing the kapp.

"More pins," she explained, reaching up again to yank each one out. Next came the hairnet and additional pins underneath it. Fixing her hair under a kapp was her least favorite chore, and she looked forward to never doing it again. She would've disposed of it earlier if her hair wasn't so long and unmanageable.

Finally, she shook out the bun and pulled the hair tie out. Cascading down to her lower back, her hair fell in waves. Outside, the wind chimes played their summer song louder, and the curtains at the open window above the sink ruffled in the breeze. Her tresses blew around her shoulders with the draft. As she stood there, a flash of wickedness took her by surprise, a longing for Mr. Foster to run his hands through her hair.

So improper.

Not for the first time, she wondered what was happening to her.

Everything inside her ached to be touched.

"I-I didn't realize your hair was so long," Mr. Foster said in a thicker-than-usual voice. His eyes, dark and intense, swept over her features. "It's quite beautiful. You're a beautiful girl, Hanna. Don't ever forget that."

No one had ever called her beautiful before, and she didn't quite know how to receive the compliment. She'd grown up learning how to be plain and proper. How to never draw attention to herself. Taking her kapp off and letting her hair down in front of an English man was an act that would've been punished severely. Now it felt wonderful and freeing, even more so because she didn't fear her daat's fist or cruel words, or having to shamefully confess her sins in front of the bishops.

"It's never been cut," she said.

"Do you want to cut it?"

A choice. Mr. Foster was giving her another choice about her appearance.

Careful to hide her giddiness, she nodded. "Yes. I couldn't bear to wear it down when it's this long, but I don't want to put the kapp back on."

"We'll get you a haircut tomorrow too. Maybe we'll spend the whole day in town. I need supplies for the garden and some other odds and ends."

Hanna agreed, then she set about finishing lunch and soon had the bacon, lettuce, and tomato sandwiches Mr. Foster had requested ready.

She joined him at the table and couldn't stop thinking about tomorrow's trip to town.

During most of her previous trips to town, she hadn't been allowed out of the buggy. In fact, she'd only been inside the Dollar General and a quilting shop a few times. After Abram and Jacob had joined the church, her father no longer paid any mind to their travels to town. She'd envied their freedom, and she was jealous her rumspringha had been restricted to nothing more than a few buggy rides with young Amish men to church or a game of volleyball with others her age. She suspected her daat was extra strict with her since she'd been indecisive the first time he'd asked if she was ready to join the church, shortly before her seventeenth birthday. He'd likely thought shielding her from the English ways would prevent her from leaving. Instead, she'd grown more curious over the years. More isolated within her tightknit community. Lonelier. More determined.

"Hanna, we need to discuss the trip to town," Mr. Foster said once he finished his lunch.

"All right."

"I get odd looks when I go to town. People think I'm strange because I live out here by myself, and most everyone thinks I'm some kind of crazy survivalist with a bunker, just waiting for the government to come take my guns away."

Half of what Mr. Foster said didn't make sense. She strived to understand his meaning, but her thoughts grew fuzzy. "A crazy survivalist? What do you mean?" Guns terrified her and she hoped he didn't own one, but fear kept her from asking.

"A weirdo," he said. "A man who has secrets. A man who has mental problems." He tapped at his head.

"I'm afraid I still don't understand."

"They don't like me because I'm different."

"Ah. I see now." She could certainly relate to being different. To not belonging.

"Anyway, Hanna, if people in town find out I'm harboring a young girl who just left the Amish community, it might mean trouble for us. They might think I'm taking advantage of you and keeping you here against your will. I don't want any do-gooders nosing around in our business."

"How will we go to town then?" Her spirits plummeted. Would he make her wait in his truck? Or worse yet, tell her he'd changed his mind?

"When we visit town, we'll pretend you're my daughter."

"You want me to call you Daat?"

"No, not *Daat*. No Amish words. *Dad* or *Daddy* will do just fine. I'm pushing forty, so I am old enough to be your father." His brown eyes darkened further as he stared at her.

"Yah. I'll call you Daddy when we go to town."

"Not yah. Yes. Say 'yes, Daddy.'"

Her face heated and the aching between her thighs pulsed hotter. She inhaled a deep, calming breath, even as her heart raced, and her face became flushed. She squirmed in her seat and finally murmured, "Yes, Daddy," as she held Mr. Foster's dark, intense gaze.

CHAPTER 4

Lingering awkwardly outside a women's dressing room, Ben waited as Hanna tried on outfit after outfit. The selection had overwhelmed her, so he'd picked out a few dresses, most of them modest in style. From what he could see of her as she'd modeled the form-fitting clothes, she'd had a beautiful, curvy body hidden underneath those plain dresses.

To fight his impending hard-on, he'd fled the dressing room area on the premise of finding her at least one pair of pants and some t-shirts.

As he fumbled through a stack of jeans, he realized she probably needed underthings too. Christ. He groaned inwardly. What the hell had he gotten himself into?

Ever since she'd arrived at his house a week ago, he'd been one giant walking erection.

"Can I help you find something, sir?"

His head shot up at the sound of a woman's voice. A sales associate. Thank God. He stood up, glancing over his shoulder at the dressing room. "Yes, um, my daughter's getting a whole new wardrobe for college. She might need help picking out... under-things." Covering his mouth, he coughed uncomfortably. "You know. Panties. Bras."

The woman, a plump redhead with a saccharine smile, raised an eyebrow. He didn't need to be psychic to read her thoughts. She obviously found it strange that a woman old enough to go to college was out shopping for bras and panties with her dad. Cringing, his mind raced for an explanation to offer the woman.

He came up empty.

"Is that her underwear size?"

Ben held a pair of jeans in his hands, the same size as the dresses. "Yes. Think so."

"What about bra size, sir?"

"Huh?"

"What's her bra size?"

"Not sure. Maybe you could bring a few sizes for her to try out?"

"Of course. I'll be back shortly." She disappeared to the other end of the store where panties and bras hung on racks.

Ben gave himself a mental shake before calling for Hanna outside the dressing room. She appeared in front of the mirrors, head inclined as she approached him.

A long, flower-patterned purple dress clung to her bosom and waist, flowing out from her hips to graze her ankles. And she definitely, most definitely, wasn't wearing a bra. A hint of her nipples showed like tiny peaks through the fabric. Jesus fucking Christ. His jeans suddenly became uncomfortably tight.

"Wear that one to lunch." The words escaped his mouth before he could think.

An hour later, he carried several bags to his truck that were filled with dresses, jeans, a few shirts, shoes, pajamas, and unmentionables. After locking up his truck, they ventured back inside the mall to a walk-in hair salon. The hairdresser suggested Hanna donate some of her long, beautiful locks to cancer patients, and Hanna readily agreed.

When it was all said and done, she'd lost fourteen inches of hair, but it was still rather long and swept over her shoulders in shining waves.

He couldn't stop staring, especially when it blew in the breeze as they exited the mall again.

"Do you like pizza?" He opened the car door, waiting for her to crawl inside.

"Yes. I've had it before. Sarah made it once, but Daat and my brothers didn't like it, so she never made it again. I've never had it from a restaurant though." She graced him with a smile as she hopped on the seat, smoothing out her dress.

"Let's go get pizza, then." He leaned over to buckle her in, then closed her door and rounded the truck, sliding in to start the engine.

"Mr. Foster?"

"Yes?" From the corner of his eye, he noticed her hands fidgeting in her lap. He turned his body to face her, puzzled over her sudden anxiety.

"Thank you for the job. Thank you for the room. Thank you for the clothes. I am so grateful for your help. You're a very good man, helping me like this." Her stark blue eyes brimmed with sincerity, and she looked achingly vulnerable at this moment.

The urge to gather her in his arms was unbearable.

He wanted to hold her and promise everything would be okay. To tell her she would grow up to have a wonderful life, despite being estranged from her biological family. He ached to soothe her fears. He also ached to possess her, to teach her pleasure and keep her with him forever. To cuddle her and take care of her the way a sweet little girl like her deserved. The thought of eventually letting her go, the thought of sending her off into the cruel world he'd once escaped, filled him with angry despair.

Though she was incredibly shy and quiet, he saw a fire burning within her. An independent streak that had been squashed by years of living under her father's overbearing authority. He was more than glad to help her overcome it.

As the silence loomed, Ben decided it wouldn't hurt to show her some physical affection.

He covered her hands with his.

Their first skin-to-skin contact.

The temperature in the truck rose ten degrees.

Panic flickered briefly in her eyes, and she surveyed the parking lot, as if to make sure no one was witnessing this semi-intimate moment.

"I'm happy to help you, Hanna. You're a good kid. You deserve the best out of life." He grinned and gave her hands a gentle squeeze, reveling in the warmth of the touch. "Besides, I enjoy your company. Helping you is no hardship to me."

She returned his smile. "I'm not a kid, Mr. Foster."

He almost sucked in a quick breath but stopped himself. Instead, he mumbled a placid response, released her hands, and drove to the pizza place while trying to fight off yet another erection.

Tony's Pizza wasn't fancy by any means, but by

the way Hanna gawked around with open wonder, it could've been a five-star restaurant.

To his surprise, she made small talk with the waitress who came to take their order, and she smiled at a few of the patrons sitting nearby.

It seemed Hanna was starting to come out of her shell, little by little.

He alone would witness her transformation.

He would help make it possible, and he felt charged with the responsibility to guide her and keep her safe.

Failing her wasn't an option.

She visited the restroom as he paid the bill. His mood was light, until three college-aged girls who reeked of marijuana and beer walked past the counter and into the same restroom. He waited and waited, wondering what was taking Hanna so long. Just as he was about to storm in after her, she emerged, laughing amidst the group of stoners.

Ben frowned as they all approached him.

"Daddy, I was wondering if I might go to a movie with Carla, Theresa, and Vicky while you run your errands?" Hanna gestured at her new *friends*.

Ben's jaw tightened. Carla, Theresa, and Vicky probably knew Hanna used to be Amish based on her accent. He hadn't taken her Dutch accent into account when he'd come up with the grand idea of pretending he was her father. No doubt these girls thought it would be funny to get Hanna high or corrupt her in some other fashion.

His teeth ground together as he glared at the three mean-spirited young women, but his countenance softened when he regarded Hanna.

"Not today, sweetheart," he said. "I need your help picking out some things."

"Oh, come on, *Daddy*," one of the girls said mockingly. "Hanna says she's new in town and doesn't have any friends. We'd love to show her around."

"Absolutely not!" His incensed tone earned him curious stares from several diners.

Hanna looked hurt and confused. Her eyes flashed. "If I want to go to a movie with someone my own age, Mr. Foster, I have a right to do so."

"Mr. Foster? I thought he was your dad?" another of the girls said. The three of them exchanged glances, giggling.

"It's time to go, Hanna. Now."

Though her face reddened and her eyes still blazed, Hanna nodded and said a quick apology to the three young women before taking a step toward Ben. Without thinking, he gripped her upper arm and guided her outside, not releasing her until they reached the truck.

"Young lady, I ought to give you a good spanking for that. I told you in town you needed to do as I say and call me Daddy. I warned you about people trying to take advantage of you. Did you not listen to a word I said? What were you thinking, arguing with me and calling me Mr. Foster in front of the whole restaurant?" He leaned down to scold her, hands braced against the car door on either side of her body, pinning her in place without actually touching her.

Lower lip trembling, she peered up at him from under thick eyelashes, her cheeks suddenly pale. "I.... I..." She fumbled to speak but soon clamped her mouth shut.

"Those girls were high as a kite, Hanna. That means they were on drugs. Couldn't you smell it? They reeked. You could get in serious trouble hanging out with a group of girls like that. You could end up in jail or worse."

"I'm sorry." Her apology came out in a shaky whisper. "I thought they were being nice to me. I-I didn't know."

As he considered the situation from her point of view, most of his anger dissipated. He couldn't hold her responsible for her naivety. He backed up, dropping his arms to his sides.

"We'll talk about it at home," he said.

As they finished the rest of their shopping, Ben

found it hard to concentrate, and Hanna avoided looking him in the eye. His threat to spank her hung between them. Her brief defiance had called up his stern, protective side.

She was his responsibility.

She was young and needed guidance.

By the time they arrived back at the cabin in the early evening, turning Hanna over his knee for a bare-bottom spanking was all he could think about.

The urge to scold her, spank her, and comfort her in his arms afterward was the strongest urge he'd had in ages.

CHAPTER 5

The tension as Hanna placed breakfast on the table almost brought her to tears. It was a relief to know she could cry again, but she couldn't abide this unease that lingered between her and Mr. Foster.

He'd lectured her last night about the dangers of the outside world, and he'd seemed the most upset that she'd argued with him in public. She felt awful. She would've never dared argue with any of her family members in public.

Shame welled up tight within her until she lost her appetite and picked at the eggs and bacon.

Acutely aware of his every move, she suffered through breakfast. He informed her that he would be working on his computers most of the day. He designed webpages for businesses, and while she wasn't quite sure what that meant, she knew he worked for long hours on the computer, sometimes staying up late past the time she retired.

A spanking.

Yesterday, in the parking lot, he'd said he should spank her. How unexpected. And terrifying. Until she'd witnessed his fury firsthand, she'd thought him to be a gentle man.

She ran a hand through her shortened hair in frustration. Even though the thought of a spanking scared her, the thought of being spanked by Mr. Foster also left her squirming.

Though she hated to experience pain, her curiosity kept growing—right alongside her guilt over disappointing him. The whole restaurant had witnessed her blatant display of disrespect.

Young lady, I ought to give you a good spanking for that...

If he spanked her, how would he do it?

Would he turn her over his knee, or would he direct her to bend over a table or a desk?

He wouldn't be cruel. A man like Mr. Foster would be loving in his punishments. Of this she was certain. He wouldn't punch or kick her in anger. He hadn't threatened to do that at all, nor had he yelled hurtful words into her ears. He wasn't a violent man.

She felt safe with Mr. Foster. She trusted him.

Would a spanking be so horrible? She

suspected it would alleviate the tension between them, and she also suspected it would ease her guilt. His quiet disapproval stung, and she wanted things set right.

Of course, she'd apologized a thousand times, but it wasn't enough for her, even if it was enough for him.

Hanna swallowed hard and rushed to find Mr. Foster before she lost her nerve.

She had never in her life craved a punishment, nor had she experienced this level of guilt over her behavior before. Yet her desire to be spanked, or whatever punishment Mr. Foster deemed appropriate, was overwhelming. As overwhelming as the walls of the farmhouse that had once suffocated her, prompting her to flee.

She tapped lightly on the door to his office. "Mr. Foster?"

The door flung open almost immediately. He stood, staring down at her, his expression unreadable. "Yes, Hanna?" His deep voice rumbled through her like a physical touch.

"I'd like to speak with you." Behind him, two large screens glowed on a wide table against the wall. Several books were stacked on an otherwise empty desk against the opposite wall. Sunlight swept across the room through an open window.

"All right. Come in." He moved aside and she entered his domain.

She took a seat on a chair he pointed at, then folded her hands in her lap and sat as straight as possible. He hovered above her, and his strong presence caused her insides to flutter.

She'd never reacted so strongly to any man before.

It was as if she were about to melt at his feet.

She was warm all over, but especially hot between her thighs, where she tingled and quaked as her anticipation grew.

"What is it, Hanna?" The deep timbre of his voice vibrated through her chest.

"I feel awful for disobeying you yesterday. I can't stop thinking about it. I-I wish you would... punish me." She dropped her gaze and concentrated on the floor. "Please."

He was silent for so long that she feared he hadn't heard her. But eventually, he spoke.

"Hanna, I don't think that would be appropriate."

She lifted her head, forcing herself to meet his eyes. "In the parking lot you said..."

"That I ought to give you a good spanking?"

Her whole body flushed, and she felt increasingly faint. "Yes."

"Is that really what you want, Hanna? You want me to spank you?"

Gulping past the soreness in her throat, she nodded and felt the heat between her legs flare up again. She watched warily as Ben paced the floor a few times.

Asking for a spanking was humiliating enough, but it would be even worse if he rejected her and sent her out of his office.

Guilt and shame would devour her slowly if that happened.

Finally, he came to a standstill in the center of the room. Her gaze traveled up his jeans, up his broad chest, and to his hard visage. Determination gleamed in his dark eyes. He looked more forbidding than she imagined he could ever appear, even more forbidding than he had in the parking lot as he'd scolded her. Truly, she was glimpsing a new side of him.

A stern side.

But beneath his sternness, he was still Mr. Foster. Her friend. He wouldn't hurt her. Not really. Not like her daat.

"Very well, Hanna. Stand up."

She followed his command, rising up on shaky legs as he drew closer until he towered above her, dwarfing her petite form. He placed a hand on her shoulder and peered directly in her face. She fought the desire to back away, as well as the desire to lean into him. To feel his arms around her.

Flustered, she waited for further instruction.

"Tell me why you're getting this spanking, young lady."

She gasped lightly at his order. "Because I disobeyed you. I argued with you in public and I deliberately called you by your name."

"That's right, Hanna. I only want what's best for you. You're living under my roof and you're under my authority. It's my job to protect you and guide you. I'm going to spank you now. I hope you learn something from it, and I hope the sting of my hand on your bottom serves to remind you to mind me in the future."

Tears flooded her vision. She blinked rapidly as she nodded her understanding.

Her heart swelled.

She'd never felt so... cared for.

She hesitated to use the word love, to think of love, because she'd never used that word before. It was an English word with no Amish equivalent, and it had never truly startled her until this moment, this moment when Mr. Foster was preparing to punish her.

And most of all, she understood this was a far cry

from her daat's typical punishment. Mr. Foster wanted to teach her a lesson, not take his anger out on her.

He released her shoulder, took a seat on the chair, and patted his leg. "Over my knee."

A single tear burned down her cheek as she moved to stand at his side. Their eyes locked before he guided her down over his lap, taking her across his sturdy thighs.

The height of the chair, combined with Mr. Foster's tall stature, prevented her toes from touching the floor. She tensed as he rested one hand on her lower back, while his other hand cupped her bottom. His touch sent a shiver up her spine. She held her breath until her chest burned.

"I'm afraid I can't allow you the protection of your skirt. Naughty girls get spanked on their bare bottoms."

"Mr. Foster! You can't!" She squirmed in protest as he flipped back the skirt of the new English dress she was wearing, tucking it around her waist. When she'd imagined him spanking her, it had been with the protection of her clothing.

"Not Mr. Foster. *Daddy*. We'll be going out in public again, and I don't want another slipup, so you will call me Daddy from now on, even at home." A single swat stung her thigh. "Settle down, Hanna.

You asked for this. Trust Daddy to give you what you need."

She froze, and he yanked her panties down to rest at her knees.

Oh no. No no no.

He could see her. Her backside was bared to him in a most humiliating position. She could feel the cool air of the room drifting over her bottom, reminding her of her nudity, her vulnerability.

Could he see anything between her legs?

At the thought, she tensed up and pressed her thighs together.

"Young lady, you will relax that bottom right now. Good girl. Now spread your legs a bit. That's it. I want you to feel every slap I give you." His deep, stern voice washed over her.

Humiliation coursed through her in sharp waves, but she did as he asked with minimal hesitation. To ease her guilt over her nudity in front of a man who wasn't her husband, she told herself she didn't have a choice in the matter.

Besides, she trusted him. If she didn't trust him, she wouldn't have asked for a spanking in the first place. How long would he spank her? Would it hurt terribly? Her breath caught in her chest, and the familiar aching sensation she frequently experienced between her thighs while in his presence returned full force.

"That's perfect. Now give me your hands."

She awkwardly reached back, only for him to pin her wrists down, holding them in the firm grip of one large hand.

"I'm going to spank you now, Hanna. Be a good girl and keep as still as possible. Don't you dare start fighting me."

Fight him? The idea hadn't crossed her mind.

But after the first slap landed on her right cheek, the searing pain of that single blow made her second-guess asking for this spanking. Her left cheek came next, and he masterfully alternated smacks between her bottom cheeks, paying equal attention to them both.

The sting built up quickly, blooming across her skin, and she couldn't help kicking her legs a few times.

She stilled when her panties fell to her ankles, determined not to lose them completely. As if holding on to the scrap of material provided her an ounce of modesty, despite the fact that it wasn't even covering her bottom. He spanked hard, even moving lower to spank the tops of her poor thighs.

Although the spanking was painful, she was glad he wasn't letting her off easy. She'd disobeyed him in public. This was a fitting punishment, exactly what she needed, just as he'd said. *Trust me to give you what you need.*

He paused to rub her punished flesh. "I'm doing this because I care about you, Hanna. I was a fool not to see it before, but even though you like your newfound freedom, you still need rules and structure in your life. I can give that to you. I want to give that to you."

As his words sank in, as well as the fact that he'd ordered her to address him as *Daddy*, he thrashed her backside with a series of quick, painful slaps that broke through her self-control and left her crying out. Sobs caused her shoulders to heave when his hand stilled again, and he soon started rubbing her tender bottom.

"Shh, little girl. It's over now. All is forgiven."

CHAPTER 6

BEN HELPED Hanna rise to her feet. She buried her face in her hands, though her crying had stopped. No doubt she couldn't look at him yet. He knelt to pull her panties up, and she was so deep in her shame that she didn't protest his familiarity with her body.

"Come here." He pried her hands away and wiped at the remainder of her tears with a tissue. "Are you all right?"

"Yah. I-I mean yes. Thank you, Mr. Fost... Daddy. Thank you, Daddy." She smiled at him through her misery.

A tremor coursed up his thighs, and desire tightened his balls when she called him Daddy. The idea had struck him in the heat of the moment, and her receptiveness to the name change pleased him.

He cupped her face, not allowing her to look

away. "I don't want to take your choices away from you, Hanna. But I do expect you to follow the few rules I have. I promise I only want to protect you. I won't let you carry around guilt, and if a spanking helps you feel better, I'll give you a spanking." If anyone understood the devastation of guilt, it was Ben.

"It did make me feel better, but I didn't expect you to..." Her words trailed off and she blushed.

"Spank your bare bottom?"

"Right. I didn't expect that."

He hadn't expected it either. He felt wicked for baring her to his gaze. At the time he'd told himself he only wanted to punish her properly, but the truth was much darker than that. He'd wanted to see her little ass turning red under his slaps. The fruits of his labor. And he'd wanted to glimpse the sweetness between her thighs as she squirmed over his lap.

He'd also wanted to slip his fingers into her wet core, but he had at least shown some restraint in that department.

This time.

"Do you wish to be spanked over your panties or over your dress next time?" he asked.

"Next time?" Her eyes widened and she appeared flustered.

"If I have to spank you again, Hanna," he said.

She gawked at him as the seconds ticked by. Outside, Lady barked and her footsteps sounded on the porch. The wind chimes clattered their familiar slow song. A gust of wind lifted the curtains and sent a few papers flying off his desk. Lost in the moment as their eyes remained locked, he waited for her answer, heart hammering in his chest.

"If you have to spank me again, I suppose it should be as it was this time. I-I trust you to give me what I need." Her eyes filled with so much trust as she gazed at him that his chest suddenly felt tight.

Bare bottom. His cock hardened and strained against his jeans. Not exactly perfect timing when he'd planned to give her a hug. But he couldn't send her away without offering her comfort. Hell, he needed it as much as she did after bringing her to tears.

"Come here. Come to Daddy." He gathered her close, tucking her head under his chin. He stroked her hair and wrapped an arm around her waist. She melted against him, circling her arms around his center and pressing her cheek to his chest.

He never wanted to release her.

If he could have stopped time, he would have done so without a second thought, even if it cost him his soul.

He leaned into her, inhaling the scent of the

shampoo they'd picked up at a drug store after leaving the pizza place yesterday. In fact, he'd gotten her all sorts of feminine toiletries he suspected she wasn't accustomed to. It occurred to him that her legs had appeared smooth and bare when he lifted her dress. Apparently, she'd used some of the stuff he'd bought her. More transformation. The shy, sheltered Amish girl was disappearing, and a beautiful, innocent woman was taking her place.

More barking from Lady broke into his reverie, and he pulled back far enough to place a kiss on Hanna's forehead. She blushed again. It appeared he pushed her limits, but it also appeared she liked it.

"No one has hugged me in years. Well, besides my little nieces and nephews. My mother was the last adult to hug me, and that was when I was five years old, right before she died."

"The Amish don't hug each other?" He'd had no idea. He was stunned.

"We do. Sometimes. But it's not allowed in public. My daat is rather rigid on the subject and doesn't encourage it at home either."

Though Hanna had grown up a few miles away, she might as well have been from another country, as different as her upbringing had been.

"Would you like to go fishing with me today?"

Hanna's face lit up. "Yes!"

"Go put on a pair of jeans and meet me in the kitchen."

He gave her backside a playful swat as she rushed out of his office. He then counted backwards from one hundred until his erection softened and his pulse returned to normal.

In the kitchen, he rooted around in the refrigerator and the cabinets for something to pack for a picnic lunch. He decided on ham sandwiches, fruit, and pasta salad.

"What are you doing?"

He turned to see Hanna standing beside the table, and her appearance caused his erection to return in the blink of an eye.

One hundred. Ninety-nine. Ninety-eight...

The jeans hugged her shapely hips, and the pink fitted t-shirt she wore accentuated the swell of her breasts. A C-cup, he mused as he recalled her size. 34C to be exact.

The perfect size as far as he was concerned. A generous handful.

His gaze roamed over her body for far too long, but he didn't care if she noticed. They were close to crossing a barrier, and even though she was young and innocent, he suspected she was smart enough to realize it.

"Your hair looks nice like that." He pointed to her

head.

She touched the ponytail. "Thank you."

His heart lurched. Instead of shying away from a compliment like usual, she'd accepted it with thanks. It was a small step, but it was still a step forward. As she stood with one hand perched on the back of a chair, gazing out the open window, she didn't even realize what she'd done.

He smiled and dug through a bottom cabinet for a small cooler. "I thought we could have a picnic by the stream today. Why don't you grab an old blanket from the hallway closet?"

"I can make lunch." Alarm touched her voice.

Ben chuckled. "I'm going to make lunch for you for a change, Hanna. Go get the blanket."

"Yes, Daddy."

Daddy. He could get used to being called that. When he turned with the packed cooler in hand, Hanna had already returned with a plaid blanket neatly tucked over her arm. She looked at him expectantly while twisting her fingers together.

He found her nervous habit of twisting her fingers together adorable, almost as cute as when she squirmed and blushed.

"Ready to go," he said. "The fishing poles are out in the shed. Worms too."

Lady greeted them outside, tail wagging and tongue lolling from her mouth.

"Wanna catch some fish, Lady?"

The dog's ears moved into perfect points and she barked, then ran circles around them as they approached one of the storage sheds. Hanna laughed and knelt with her hand outstretched while Ben slipped inside the shed. When he returned with their fishing gear, Lady was sprawled out in the grass getting her tummy scratched by Hanna.

"Get up, Lady, there's fish to catch!" As Ben expected, the dog shot to her feet and started barking again. The word 'fish' usually did the trick. Lady always benefited from a fishing trip as much as Ben did. She liked her fish fried in butter with a dash of lemon juice.

"I take it Lady's been fishing before?" Hanna asked with a bright smile. The wind picked up her hair, blowing her ponytail this way and that.

"Lady's an expert. Aren't you, girl?"

The German Shepherd barreled around the cabin to the beginning of a path they'd worn down over the years. Ben explained to Hanna that it led to a clearing that bloomed with wildflowers every spring. "The creek is right beyond the clearing." A few times since her arrival, he'd gone fishing in the mornings and brought home trout for dinner. The first time he'd instructed her to fry up a fish just for Lady, the look on her face had been priceless.

"How long have you lived out here?" Hanna shifted the blanket to her other arm.

"Eight years." He focused on the path, not wishing to encourage her to ask another question that might lead to more inquiries about his past. He had his reasons for living in the backwoods of Pennsylvania.

"Why?" She peered at him with a curious gleam in her eyes.

"Excuse me?" Unease spread through him.

"Why do you live out here all alone?" she asked.

He squinted as a shaft of sunlight pierced through the trees. "Same reason you left your home. I didn't belong anymore."

A vague answer. But it was the only answer he could give her. If she knew about his past, she might view him differently. Whether she would feel sorry for him or simply be appalled by his history, he wasn't certain.

It was a risk he wasn't willing to take. At least not yet.

CHAPTER 7

THE SMELL of frying fish filled the kitchen. Lady sat impatiently at Hanna's feet, tail wagging in anticipation of dinner. Ben had been in his office since they arrived back at the cabin with a fine catch of five medium-size trout.

Hanna had enjoyed their morning and afternoon spent together. She shivered with excitement, recalling the feel of his body pressing against hers as he guided her to cast the pole.

She closed her eyes, savoring the delicious flood of memories. His warm, callused hands on hers. The accidental brush of his stubble on her cheek. The unstoppable flutters in her belly.

The pulses of warm delight between her thighs.

What *was* that, anyway?

She put the thoughts aside, tucking them away to reexamine another time and concentrated on dinner.

Later that night, as she was brushing out her damp, freshly-washed hair, a knock on her door startled her. Ben had never visited her in her room, though it was located directly beside his. Her heart raced and her palms became sweaty. She threw the hairbrush on the bed, wiped her hands on her pajama shorts, and hurried to open the door.

"Good evening, Da-Daddy. Did you need something?" She peered up at him, slightly embarrassed over her stuttering of his new title, and instantly became lost in his dark, beautiful eyes. Often when she gazed into those depths, her throat constricted and her insides shook with a longing she couldn't reconcile.

To want a man this way must be indecent.

But she wanted him so much that she wondered if being decent mattered anymore.

Urges she ached to quench plagued her day and night.

Constant throbbing. Constant restlessness.

It was as if she were ill, but only his touch could cure her condition.

How to proceed with her urges was a challenge she wasn't brave enough to face. Yet. At least not without a sign of equal desire from Mr. Foster. Daddy.

Did he ache for her too?

Did he toss and turn in bed, losing sleep over his cravings?

"Would you like to watch a movie?" he asked, and his intense gaze penetrated deep, making her feel increasingly flustered. "I can make popcorn."

"A movie? On the television?" She'd spotted a large television in the living room, but she hadn't seen him turn it on once since her arrival. Though she'd been curious, she hadn't toyed with the device, even when she'd been alone in the house. Especially after her incident in town. She'd asked to go to a movie and ended up earning a spanking over her behavior.

Her eyes fell to his large hands as the memories came rushing back.

Those hands...

Firm, yet gentle. Caring.

"Yes, on the television." A smile touched his voice.

"All right." She beamed at him, eager to spend the evening at his side.

"My movie collection isn't very large. Why don't you pick something off the shelf?"

Not only was she going to spend the evening

with Mr. Foster, but she was going to watch her first movie. Thrilled beyond measure, she followed him to the cozy living room. She inspected the movies lined up on a shelf next to the television.

After several minutes of inspecting the covers, she glanced up at Mr. Foster, feeling a bit overwhelmed.

"There's so many to choose from. How do I decide?" It was like she was back in the mall, staring at rows and stacks of clothing. Too many choices scared her sometimes, and she hated this weakness inside her. Would it ever leave? Would the world she'd longed to join always feel so large and intimidating? The world she'd left had been suffocating, and all she wanted was a middle ground that included the freedom to make her own decisions.

He gave her a patient smile. "How about a musical?" His chest pressed against her arm as he reached for a movie. A warm puff of breath hit her cheek, and the scent of his soap tantalized her. Pine? Eucalyptus? He moved away too quickly, though his delicious masculine scent lingered, and she found herself wishing he would brush his body against her again.

"Sure," she said, trying out an English word she hadn't used yet. Mr. Foster said it was a casual *yes,* whatever that meant. It felt strange on her tongue.

"Here, let me show you how this works." He

knelt and reached toward a black box beneath the television.

She tried to concentrate as he explained how the DVD player worked. Press this button. Press that button. Wait for a few seconds. Grab the remote. Press more buttons. Wait some more. It was much harder than learning to use the washing machine and dryer. To his credit, he was patient and repeated the instructions three times until she was finally able to do it without his assistance. He promised to teach her how to use a computer soon too, saying it was necessary for her to complete her G.E.D. work.

"This was my mother's favorite movie," he said as they took a seat on the couch. His leg rested a mere inch from hers. He glanced down at her bare thigh, and she suddenly felt self-conscious over the shorts she was wearing.

"Are you cold?" he asked.

"A little."

To her pleasure, he produced a warm fleece blanket and brought it over her lap. He maintained eye contact as he tucked her in, smoothing his hands over the contours of her body.

Oh goodness...

Her senses heightened as time slowed down, and she found herself staring at his lips for far too long, wondering what it might be like if he kissed her. Her entire body flushed with warmth at the thought, and when she pressed her thighs together, the pulses in her core became so heightened that she almost whimpered.

"As snug as a bug," he murmured, oh so close to her ear. "Say 'thank you, Daddy.'"

Her breath caught in her throat, and she stared back at him with wide eyes. "Th... thank you, Daddy."

She tingled all over and wished he was tucked under the blanket with her. He could wrap one huge, muscular arm around her, pull her close, press his body against hers, and... and...

What then? Something. She was hot all over at once, sweltering in the confines of the blanket, yet she couldn't throw it off and appear silly and indecisive. *I'm cold. Oh, never mind. I'm really hot.*

"I love your hair, Hanna. I must admit I can't stop admiring it. So long, so wavy." He reached out to stroke a strand between his fingers.

She became instantly lightheaded. Her lips parted in surprise, and for a brief moment she thought he might actually kiss her. Disappointment surged through her when he didn't.

If she was good, if she was proper, she would run out the door and back to the farm.

But Hanna wasn't good and proper any longer.

She was becoming a new person. A person who looked at the world with eyes wide open, even though she hadn't seen much of the world yet.

Right now, Mr. Foster was a big part of her world. He was her only friend, and in a way, he was her whole world. Loving, but strict.

She'd thought she would never want to be under the authority of anyone, yet she had never been happier than now.

Even if he spanked her again, and a small part of her hoped he would, she would always treasure her time with him. For however long a time they had together.

Eli had stayed two years. A month hadn't passed yet since her arrival here, and she took comfort in knowing that he wouldn't pressure her to leave anytime soon. Not that she ever pictured him pressuring her to leave.

Would he allow her to remain here in his cabin forever, in exchange for her moderate chores?

No, she couldn't think of it. She wanted to see more of the world, didn't she? To leave Pennsylvania far behind one day? To get an education, find a job, and secure her independence?

The farm was only a few miles away, and the proximity of it haunted her. It was a shadow she could only escape by putting a few states between her and the entire community she'd once belonged to.

The movie started, but Hanna had a hard time concentrating on it with Mr. Foster by her side. He ran off to make popcorn shortly after the opening. When their hands touched in the popcorn bowl, the frustrating pleasure surging between her thighs flamed and tightened. Every touch and every glance affected her in ways she was beginning to enjoy more and more, despite her confusion.

She squirmed as the achiness built, and her panties grew moist. She suspected there was a connection between the two—the aching and the wet state of her panties.

This wasn't the first time she'd soaked a pair of panties in Mr. Foster's presence.

"Still cold?" he asked.

Oh, dear. He'd mistaken her squirming for shivering.

Hanna nodded, though she was far from cold. But he couldn't learn of the sensations driving through her, or the moisture pooling in her panties. She wasn't ready to be so bold yet.

He placed the popcorn bowl on a table and stared at her for a long moment. "Come here, little girl."

CHAPTER 8

Ben scooted closer to Hanna and wrapped an arm around her shoulders. He'd noticed her shivering, and he'd also noticed the flushing of her cheeks. Perhaps she was getting sick. Maybe she'd picked up a bug during the trip to town.

"Do you feel all right?" He placed a hand on her forehead. Hot to the touch. Feverish for sure.

"Yes, Daddy. I feel fine."

"No, you don't. You're burning up." He turned to inspect her further. Alarm and concern rushed through him. "When did this start?"

Her eyes widened. "When did *what* start?"

"The shivering. The fever." He placed the back of his hand to her head again. Definitely feverish. Her illness roused his protective side once more.

He would take care of her. He would make sure she got better.

"I'm not shivering, and I don't have a fever," she said in an adamant tone.

He arched an eyebrow, not quite believing. He pulled the blanket away and frowned. Sweat glistened on her arms and dampened her shirt. "I don't like being lied to, Hanna. I can see that you're feeling sick. Why didn't you tell me?"

Her eyes narrowed. "I'm not sick and I would appreciate you leaving me alone. Can we please just watch the movie?"

In response to her agitation, he grabbed the remote and turned the TV off. "No." His voice was firm. "Stay here and don't move. I'm going to find a thermometer."

Annoyance flashed over her features, and she soon crossed her arms. Though he was worried for her health, he almost grinned at her indignant display. She was behaving like a naughty little girl.

If she didn't check her attitude, she would find herself over her daddy's lap getting her bare bottom smacked.

The digital thermometer he stored in his bathroom was dead. He doubted he had the correct battery to replace it, so he grabbed a basic oral thermometer, knowing it would work just fine—if he could get Hanna to sit still for three minutes.

When he returned to the living room, she wasn't anywhere to be seen. The blanket rested in the middle of the floor, as if she'd dropped it in the midst of a hasty escape. His right palm twitched.

"Hanna!" Irritated over her disobedience, he stalked to her bedroom.

"I'm not sick, Mr. Foster. Please go away," she called out.

"I told you to stay on the couch, young lady. And that's Daddy to you, not Mr. Foster," he said as he stood outside her bedroom door. "Do you want to be in trouble, little girl?"

"I told you to leave me alone," she said.

His temper rose at her words. "I'm coming in now," he called. He turned the knob, thankful it didn't have a lock on it. There wasn't any use for locks in the house when he lived alone.

Hanna glared at him from the bed, and her startled eyes followed him as he approached. She scooted under the sheets and yanked the covers up to her neck, shaking her head back and forth in protest.

"I'm going to take your temperature and I would appreciate your cooperation," he said. "No more running away." He held up the thermometer. "This needs to go under your tongue for three minutes."

She shook her head back and forth quickly as her hair flipped about her shoulders. Damn, she wasn't going to make this easy. He grabbed her chin and pressed the tip of the thermometer between her lips. She jerked back and tried to scramble off the bed.

"Hanna," he warned, circling an arm around her waist. "If I have to spank you to make you calm down, I won't hesitate to do it."

She froze. "I am not sick. I know I don't have a fever."

"Fine. Humor me then and open your mouth." God, he wanted to tell her to open her mouth to receive something else, but he couldn't think about that right now.

Why did her lips have to be so full and pink, so goddamn inviting?

"I will not." She struggled against his hold and pushed down on his arm.

Ben laid the thermometer on the nightstand and pulled Hanna over his lap. He'd had enough of her arguing and disobedience. She was under his roof, and it wasn't as if he hadn't warned her what would happen if she didn't behave.

She'd also agreed to his discipline after her first spanking—a spanking she'd asked for.

He covered her legs with one of his to prevent her kicking. In a matter of seconds, her flailing hands were captured and pressed to the small of her back. She was so petite it wasn't hard to trap her, though to her credit she did put up a good fight.

Her pajama shorts rode up as she squirmed, and he wasted no time in placing a volley of sharp slaps to her exposed upper thighs.

"I believe the rule in this house is that naughty girls get spanked on their bare bottoms," he said, yanking down her shorts and panties.

"No, Daddy! Please don't! Not on my bare bottom!"

Ignoring her cries, he delivered over a dozen swift smacks, spreading the punishment out evenly between both her quivering cheeks.

The sight of her flesh reddening under his hand was exquisite. He couldn't deny that there was a part of him that enjoyed punishing her, enjoyed the act of exercising his authority over her.

Not because he was cruel and wished to cause her pain, but because he cared about her and wished to provide her with guidance. He couldn't help that the act of spanking her bare bottom was erotic, though he doubted she viewed it as anything but plain punishment.

He paused to rub her cheeks when she calmed a bit, her futile kicks and squirms ceasing. Her breaths came ragged and rough, but he didn't think she was crying yet. If he had to take her to that place to secure her obedience, he would do it in a heartbeat.

He'd promised to give her what she needed, and that was what he planned to do right now, even though she might not appreciate it yet.

"Are you ready to be a good little girl?"

She didn't utter a word, but her silence spoke of anger, and he could feel the waves of insolence that radiated off her little form. His baby girl needed more spanking.

"All right then. I can see more punishment is in order." He whacked her bare bottom cheeks as she resumed squirming around in a vain effort to escape the punishing blows. He kept spanking until she was gasping for breath and promising to be a good girl. He slid her off his lap, and she immediately turned over in the bed, struggling to pull up her panties and shorts.

Confusion played across her face, and her lips formed in a prominent pout.

"I'm not sick," she said, rubbing her bottom. "You're being unreasonable."

He almost laughed at that. The only one being unreasonable was the naughty girl who obviously needed to spend more time over his knee. But he had an item to retrieve first. "I need to go get something, Hanna. I'll be right back. If you move a muscle, I'll spank you with a wooden spoon. Do you understand?"

Eyes glistening, she nodded.

"I want to hear you say, 'yes, Daddy, I understand.'"

"Yes, Daddy, I understand." Her tone was softer, but a small spark of insolence still burned through her response.

Back in his bathroom, Ben grabbed a hand towel and searched for a container of Vaseline.

Hanna needed more discipline, and it was his job to give it to her.

She would submit to the thermometer, and he no longer planned to place it under her tongue. That ship had sailed.

Determination lanced through him as he opened Hanna's bedroom door and found her still on the bed. Smart girl.

"Lie down on your stomach, little girl. It's time to take your temperature."

CHAPTER 9

"I don't understand. Why must I lie down on my stomach? I thought that's supposed to go in my mouth?" Her troubled, innocent expression made her appear younger. Locks of silky golden hair rested around her shoulders in disarray, and her cheeks were eternally flushed. God, he loved it when she blushed.

"I'm trying to help you, Hanna, and you've been quite the naughty little girl. Naughty little girls get their temperatures taken in their bottom holes."

All the color drained from her face, every last shade of pink that had stained her cheeks a moment ago disappearing in a flash. As she shook her head, her hair flipped about her face. "You can't be serious."

"Oh, but I am. Turn over on your stomach. Now.

Or I'll leave and return with a wooden spoon." His cock shifted at the prospect of smacking her bottom with a spoon as he imagined the way she would squirm and cry out as she tried to dodge the punishing blows. She would likely beg him to stop, too. *Please, Daddy.* Suddenly the room felt unbearably hot.

She took a deep breath and slowly moved into position, lying down on her stomach overtop the covers. Though her shorts were back in place, he saw evidence of her recent spanking on the backs of her thighs. The sight caused his cock to harden further, and his balls felt heavier and tighter with each breath. If he didn't pluck the temptation before him tonight, it would be a miracle. He schooled his features to be stern and approached her to take a seat on the bed next to her.

He placed a hand on her bottom. "All you had to do was obey me and stay on the couch and allow me to take your temperature. I would be done by now had you not thrown a fit, and I wouldn't have had to place it in your tight little bottom hole either. You asked for this punishment, young lady. Now be a good girl for me."

"I'm sorry, Daddy. I just really didn't want you to take my temperature."

"Why not?"

"Because I know I don't have a fever."

"Let's find out," he said, reaching for the thermometer. He placed it, along with the Vaseline and towel, down on the bed beside her. "But first I think you need a few more spanks. I'm not happy that you left the living room. I sincerely hope you learn to follow instructions better."

"Yes, Daddy," she whispered into the covers. "I'm sorry I fought you."

He dragged her shorts and panties down together until they bunched above her knees. She had the cutest little bottom. He caressed her reddened cheeks for several seconds, hoping his attentions calmed her and reminded her of the trust she'd placed in him by consenting to his discipline.

A sigh left her throat, causing him to wonder if she enjoyed his touch. He gave himself a mental shake. He'd promised her a few more spanks.

Smack! He brought his hand down sharply on her flesh, over and over. She gasped with each blow, but she didn't attempt to rise up. Such a good girl, he thought. After a dozen strikes, he resumed massaging her buttocks with one hand while he reached for the Vaseline.

"Have you had your temperature taken this way before?" he asked.

"No." She peered over her shoulder, watching as he uncapped the container.

He scooped a dollop of ointment onto his finger. "I want you to be my good girl for this part." He arched an eyebrow, and she settled back down on the bed, burying her face in the covers.

Her hands curled into tiny fists and her whole body tensed. Ben took way too much pleasure in splaying her ass cheeks apart to expose her tight hole. He also spread her much wider than necessary. Fuck, he was ready to explode in his pants. Ready to press her down and fuck that tight hole. But he couldn't. Even if Hanna wasn't sick, he couldn't act on such roguish impulses, and her well-being was far more important than his.

"I'm going to moisten you now. Be very still. This will help the thermometer ease inside you without hurting. I don't want to hurt you."

With that, he placed the ointment to her rosebud.

"Oh!" She shifted her hips but remained in place.

Ben coated her opening, taking his time to spread the Vaseline all over until it glistened over her pink puckering skin. "You're being a very good girl, Hanna."

He wiped his hand on the towel and reached for the thermometer. He spread her cheeks apart with one hand and placed the tip to her most secret entrance. Her hole clenched and unclenched as he slid it inside. When it was fully seated, he let her cheeks close and remained near her with a possessive hand on her backside, lest she decide to reach back and pull the thermometer out.

"Three minutes," he announced.

Three long minutes was more like it.

He wasn't sure if he blinked once.

His eyes refused to leave the lovely sight before him: Hanna laying stomach-down on the bed with a thermometer poking out of her freshly spanked bottom. How he ached to sink within her depths, to stroke her pink pussy, to teach her all about pleasure; preferably after he'd reddened her backside. Disciplining her awakened his primal side, the side of him that burned for her more each day, as well as the side of him that liked playing daddy to her baby girl.

He glanced at the clock on the nightstand.

"Time's up."

Once again, he spread her cheeks much wider than necessary. Her pussy was perfect, and he suspected she'd trimmed herself down there. Where she'd gotten that idea, he didn't know. The pinkness between her downy lips protruded, and as he spread her even wider, he swore he saw wetness.

Correction. A lot of wetness.

His little girl was drenched.

Stunned, he gazed at her pink parts. "Move your legs apart," he said. "Daddy needs to get a better look at you."

She obeyed without question. So willing to please.

Well, at least she was after a sound spanking.

Her pussy lips opened further to his inspection. Telltale moisture gleamed within her folds. She was beautiful and hot. Damn. Was this her problem? Maybe she didn't have a fever after all.

Realization dawned as he withdrew the thermometer from her pucker, appreciating the way her little hole winked as he dragged it out slowly.

He inspected the thermometer. No fever. "Sit up so we can talk, Hanna. Don't pull your shorts and panties up yet." How in good conscience could he leave her, frustrated and naïve as she was? Someone had to teach her. Someone had to explain why she was so wet and hot all over.

She turned over and brought her knees up to her chest, but placed one hand over her pussy in an attempt to conceal her privates. Never mind that he'd just seen *everything*. With her head inclined, she stared at the bedcovers.

It boosted his ego that she'd grown wet because of him. He doubted the movie had had anything to do with it. He took a calming breath and cleared his throat.

"You don't have a fever, Hanna. You're sexually aroused."

Her head shot up. Alarm flickered in her eyes. "Wh... what?"

"You're turned on. The reason you're all hot and bothered is because..." His voice trailed off and he waited for her reaction, hoping she would understand.

"I-I think I know what you're trying to say, and I want you to know how sorry I am. I am so ashamed." She bowed her head and her lower lip trembled.

He reached for the hand that wasn't covering her pussy. "You have nothing to apologize for, and please don't feel ashamed. What you're experiencing is perfectly normal. It's your body's natural response to..."

"To you," she finished for him. "You do this to me, don't you?"

He choked up, fumbling for words. "I didn't do it on purpose, Hanna. But I am very, very flattered."

"How do I make it stop? I feel like I'm going to die," she said as her eyes grew wider. "I'm so unsettled I can't stand it."

"Have you ever touched yourself down there before?"

"No, why would I touch myself?" Genuine confusion shone in her eyes.

"I swear I won't take advantage of you, but if you trust me enough, I'll show how to put the fire out." He ground his teeth together at the stupid analogy. "I'll show you how to make the aching feel better." There. That sounded better.

She bit her bottom lip and glanced around the room, looking uncertain, but also... tempted. Finally, she met his gaze and said, "Very well. I trust you. Please help me, Daddy."

He stared at her, trying to figure out the best way to proceed. He was honored that she trusted him enough to ask for his help.

"Give me your shorts and panties." He held out a hand as she removed them from around her ankles. Their fingers grazed as he accepted the bundle. He set the clothing aside and beckoned her to bring her legs down. "Don't be shy. I promise not to hurt you."

CHAPTER 10

Hanna's insides quaked. She bit her lip, waiting for Mr. Foster to make a move. The look in his eyes had her ready to come undone. Those dark eyes of his flashed with an emotion she didn't quite understand, but she was drawn to it. Drawn to him.

Never in her wildest dreams had she imagined he would see her naked. She might still have her shirt on, but she felt entirely naked. Shame heated her skin all over, and she tried to push the emotion away. If this was a sin, she didn't care. Besides, he was going to help her. Sweat covered her arms and legs, and she was panting with a thirst she didn't know how to quench.

The bed dipped as Mr. Foster—Daddy—sat down beside her. Her heartbeat picked up, and her breathing became even more irregular. She squirmed, waiting and waiting for his touch, for his help. Anticipation hummed through her.

"Part your legs. I want to see you." His hand grazed her thigh, but he didn't touch her between her legs.

Hanna spread her thighs and hoped Daddy approved. Her heart fluttered. She liked calling him Daddy, liked thinking of him as her loving protector in all things.

Surrendering and allowing him to take care of her was a seductive thought.

She opened her legs further and delighted in the approval that spread over his handsome features.

"That's a good girl." He brushed his fingers up her leg. "I'm going to touch you now, Hanna, and demonstrate how you can touch yourself to relieve the aching sensation you're experiencing. I'm not leaving this room until you orgasm at least twice." His voice was husky, his gaze intense.

"Or-orgasm?" She nearly choked on the word. She'd heard it in whisperings at school, and even though she hadn't understood, she'd always suspected it referred to something sexual.

"Yes."

With wide eyes, she watched as his hand edged closer to her womanly parts, to her throbbing center. She raised her hips to meet his hand and gasped. The first touch of his fingers upon her slick folds sent electric pulses throughout her body. Her nipples immediately tightened within the confines of her shirt, tightening so hard she had to resist the instinct to grasp her breasts to quell the burn of those sensitized peaks chafing against the fabric.

"Let your body guide you, Hanna. Move against my hand. Good girl. Just like that."

She pressed into his delving fingers, moving her hips up and down slowly as a delicious pressure built in her center. So much pressure. A groan escaped her when he swirled two fingers around, not quite inside her, but eliciting new waves of pleasure, sharper than ever.

"Look at me, little girl."

She opened her eyes, though she couldn't recall when exactly she'd closed them. Her heart melted at the heated, focused look on Mr. Foster's—no, Daddy's—face.

Thinking of him as her daddy, her strict but loving daddy, caused her insides to flutter.

She wanted this. Wanted him.

Wanted to be his little girl.

Wanted to be cuddled, loved, taken care of, and even spanked when she was naughty.

She moaned and thrust her center harder against

his fingers. The look of approval on his face increased and he stilled his movements.

"I think you're close to a release, Hanna. Before you come though, I want to test your control. Be a good girl and lie very still while I touch you. I mean it. Don't move a muscle. If you do, Daddy will have to punish you."

Frustrated whimpers drifted up from her, but she spread her legs wider at his bidding and tensed in anticipation of his touch.

He dipped two fingers into her pooling moisture and brought that wetness up to the tight bud he'd been working earlier, the part of her where her pleasure seemed to gather and spread outward.

Heat and friction built between his fingers and her wet center as he began to swirl over her sensitive, aching area once more.

She wasn't terribly afraid of his threat to punish her if she moved, but she desired to please him in every way possible, so she closed her eyes and concentrated on not moving. Concentrated on being his good little girl.

Smack! A light blow stung the inside of her thigh.

She opened her eyes to see Daddy wearing a scolding look.

"I didn't say you could close your eyes now, did I?" he asked.

Her gaze flitted around the room before coming to rest on him again. "No, Daddy. I'm sorry."

"Keep your eyes on me, little girl. Watch what Daddy's doing to you. Watch how Daddy is touching you."

She glanced down at the hand he had between her thighs. He drew back a moment, holding his two fingers in the air in demonstration, before plunging them back to her throbbing, quivering parts. She thrust up to meet him, momentarily forgetting that she wasn't allowed to move. Alarm filled her as she realized her error, and the dark gleam in Daddy's eyes revealed her naughtiness hadn't escaped him.

Her heart pounded.

She was in trouble with Daddy.

Would he pause in the midst of pleasuring her in this new, delightful way, to administer a punishment?

Would he actually spank her, and then go straight back to touching the slickness of her aching, inner core?

He shook his head slowly in a show of displeasure, looking especially stern, then sat back on the bed. "Did I say you could move, young lady?" he asked in a firm tone that sent delicious ripples of heat through her nerve endings.

Heat engulfed her face, the flames traveling south over the swell of her breasts, and lower to collide with the ceaseless tremors of her arousal. "No, Daddy."

"When I tell you to do something, or not to do something, however small a command it may seem, I expect your obedience. I have to spank you now, Hanna. To teach you a lesson."

His scolding and pronouncement that she was to be punished had her center pulsing in anticipation, and more moisture trickled between her thighs. She licked her lips as her heart pounded and pounded in her chest, and her legs trembled like leaves in the wind.

Before she could try to understand the cascade of emotions and sensations, Daddy lifted her up and pulled her over his lap.

His large, warm hand cupped her bottom cheeks, and she held her breath, waiting for that first slap.

"Spread those legs a bit, Hanna."

She exhaled shakily and did as he asked, parting her thighs. Her center, which felt impossibly swollen and needy, was now on display to Daddy.

A month ago, even a week ago, this position would've brought her great shame. So much shame that she would've done anything to escape it. But not today. A small amount of humiliation descended upon her, but it was nothing compared to the desire that raced through her veins.

Whatever Daddy was doing to her, she wanted more of it.

"Your bottom is already red from the spanking you received earlier," he said, massaging her cheeks. His other hand pressed against her lower back, holding her in place. "Did the thermometer hurt your bottom hole, Hanna?"

"No, it's fine," she blurted out, fearing he would touch her most private spot again.

As if reading her mind, Daddy did just that. He splayed her cheeks apart and trailed a finger down her crevice to nudge at her bottom hole. She tensed up in an attempt to deter him from pressing inside. She had no such luck.

Thick and intrusive, his finger filled her and stretched her little hole with the slight burn of his entrance.

Her mind whirled.

He was *inside* her bottom hole.

She held her breath until he stilled within her tightness. Dread mixed with heady anticipation. She wanted him to thrust his finger in and out, to feel the slight burn as she tensed against his movements. But she also wanted him to leave her bottom hole alone and just get the spanking over with.

He'd promised her pleasure, and the urgency she'd felt moments ago between her thighs increased with each gasping breath. Her breasts ached and tingled, and her nipples felt impossibly tight. She was so unsettled she could hardly stand it. She needed relief and she needed it now. Desperately so. She needed Daddy to make the aching feel better.

"Ah!" She jolted when he touched her swollen, sensitive nub. A part of her she hadn't realized existed until he'd paid it attention.

"You're going to come just like this, little girl. Right over Daddy's lap with a finger in your bottom hole."

Heat infused her face at his words. So naughty and coarse.

She spread her legs wider and gulped hard.

Slowly, he moved his finger in and out of her bottom hole.

Hard. Harder. Deeper and faster.

Tension coiled in her feminine core as he slid her moisture around her sensitive spot, swirling and applying just the right amount of pressure to...

"Oh, Daddy!" She cried out and bucked over his lap. Sensation gripped her, rolling through her in wave after wave of pulsing ecstasy. It was unlike anything she'd ever experienced before, unlike anything she'd believed was possible. She gripped the covers, tearing at them as she came undone.

"That's one," he said, his voice husky and deep.

"One?" She gasped the question.

"One orgasm. I promised you two, remember?" He withdrew his finger from her bottom and patted her thigh. The pressure of his intrusive finger lingered, a phantom pulse in her forbidden hole. "But first you're getting that spanking. You were naughty, Hanna."

"I know, Daddy," she murmured, lowering her head, though she peeked up at him from under her lashes.

"What will you do next time Daddy asks you to remain still?" he asked, lifting one eyebrow at her, and his stern expression made her tummy flutter with excitement and her privates gush with moisture.

"I... uh... I won't move."

He continued rubbing, and she wished his hand would travel lower to circle her tight bud. Despite her release moments ago, she was already aching to grind against his lap and wasn't certain how much longer she could maintain control of her urges. He'd unleashed something primal inside her and she liked it. Liked it a lot.

"That's right. You won't move unless you have permission. I'm going to spank you now, Hanna, to teach you that there are consequences when you disobey. Naughty little girls get spanked on their bare bottoms, don't they?"

"Yes."

He smacked her bottom sharply. "Yes, what?"

"Yes, Daddy."

"If you would've remained still as I'd asked, you would be enjoying another orgasm right now, Hanna. But instead, I have to spank you, and when you do finally have your second orgasm, it'll be with a very sore, very bright red little bottom."

He brought his hand down with a resounding slap, striking the lower curve of her right cheek. She gasped and squirmed on his lap, knowing the second smack would fall at any moment.

He didn't make her wait long.

The next blow impacted upon her already tender flesh, carrying more sting than the first, and he continued on without pause, alternating from right cheek to left cheek.

He covered her backside from top to bottom.

When he set into her thighs with a sharp round of smacks, she kicked her legs and writhed on his lap. The pain blazed across her flesh, spreading all over until her entire bottom burned in agony. Just as tears blurred in her eyes, the spanking stopped.

She found herself seated on Daddy's lap, strong arms circling her as he held her in his loving embrace. Soothing words reached her ears as he stroked her hair, and she wrapped her arms around his waist, leaning into his solid chest as she accepted the comfort he was offering.

As her breathing calmed, she became aware of the beating of his heart, directly at her ear. She smiled and closed her eyes. Even though she didn't know much about the world, she knew with every beat of his heart that there was nowhere else she would rather be at this moment.

Later, when he pushed her back on the bed and urged her legs apart, she didn't resist.

She obeyed when he instructed her to remain still. She thrust her hips wantonly against his fingers when he told her to let go and surrender to her urges. And when she let go, a thunderous pleasure quaked in her center and spread outward through every inch of her body until her toes curled. She floated on another plane of existence, a place where millions of stars swam in her head.

CHAPTER 11

HANNA WAS IN THE KITCHEN, emptying the dishwasher, when she heard footsteps coming from down the hallway. A thrill rushed through her, knowing Mr. Foster—Daddy—was approaching. Her pulse picked up and excitement churned in her tummy. Heated pulses also suddenly affected her between her thighs as she recalled all that had happened between them yesterday.

He'd spanked her (several times), touched her bottom hole, and caressed her privates and given her an orgasm. While she'd been over his lap getting a spanking, she could've sworn she felt something big and hard in his pants. She thought she knew what that meant but wasn't entirely certain, but she hoped she was correct—she hoped it meant Daddy desired her. That he was attracted to her. Her heart fluttered at the possibility.

She finished putting the clean plates away in the cabinets, then turned just as his huge muscular form filled the kitchen doorway. Her mouth went dry, and she found herself struggling to take in air. He was so ruggedly handsome that sometimes it took her breath away.

"It's getting late, Hanna," he said. "You ought to be in bed right now."

She flushed at the scolding tone in his voice. "Oh, I-I was planning to go to bed soon. Right after I finished putting the dishes away. And I just finished, so I suppose I'm headed to bed right now." Her face heated further. She was rambling and her heart wouldn't cease thundering in her ears.

She couldn't help but wonder if Daddy would visit her bedroom tonight? Was that how he'd known she wasn't in bed yet? He'd gone to her room looking for her?

He cleared his throat, stepped into the kitchen, and gave her a heated look. The longer he stared at her, the darker his eyes grew. "Go get ready for bed, little one. Once you have your pajamas on and you're in bed, I'll come see to your needs and then tuck you in for the night."

See to her needs? Tuck her in?

Oh Goodness. That sounded promising.

She nodded and hurried to remove her apron. "Yes, Daddy."

As she excited the kitchen, he guided her into the hallway with a hand at her lower back. But he lingered behind then and didn't follow her.

She scurried to her bedroom and got ready as fast as possible. She took a quick shower, brushed her teeth, and donned one of the short pajama dresses he'd bought her. It was a frilly garment that made her feel pretty when she put it on. When it came to putting on panties, she hesitated. Should she forgo wearing underwear to bed?

In the end, she picked a pair of panties that matched the pink nightdress and put them on. Not wearing any undergarments seemed downright scandalous, even though she knew Daddy would need to reach the parts of her they covered up.

She crawled into bed and got under the sheets. Then she waited, eagerly anticipating Daddy's arrival so he could tend to her needs. Butterflies danced in her tummy and heat commenced pulsing between her thighs. She lifted the covers and stared down at her center, spreading her legs a bit as she did so. She reached down and touched herself over her panties. Sensation shot outward and her legs trembled. A little moan escaped her throat. *Oh my.*

"Getting started without me, young lady?" came a deep voice from the doorway.

She gasped and immediately withdrew her hand from under the covers, then sat straighter against the pillows and laced her fingers together upon her lap, attempting to look contrite. Shame heated her face.

Daddy had caught her touching herself.

Was he displeased? She couldn't tell from the expression on his face. He looked a bit stern at the moment, but he also looked... excited. There was no mistaking the heat that flamed in his eyes as he entered the room.

When she glanced at his crotch, she glimpsed a definite bulge in his gray sweatpants.

He sat beside her and drew the covers back. Her breath caught in her throat at his nearness. He must've taken a quick shower, too, she realized. His hair was damp, and he smelled divine. He wore a snug white t-shirt that accentuated his muscles. Was this what he normally wore to bed? A t-shirt and sweatpants? Or did he prefer to sleep in his underwear? Her cheeks blazed as she imagined him with a lot less clothes on than he was wearing now.

He placed a hand on her thigh and pushed her nightdress up. Then he stroked two fingers along her aching center overtop the thin fabric of her panties.

She whimpered and arched into his touch. His eyes darkened further.

"If you leave these on for much longer, little girl," he said, "they'll become so soaking wet that you'll need a new pair. We'd better get them off."

She sucked in a quick breath. "Okay, Daddy."

His fingers moved to the waistband of her panties, and she lifted her hips as he pulled them off. He folded them neatly and placed them on the nightstand.

"Now," he said, "spread those legs. Show Daddy your privates."

His words sent a heady thrill through her. She nodded and slowly moved her thighs apart, revealing her nether folds to him. She could feel her moisture growing and when she glanced down, she saw a glimmer of wetness.

"So pretty and pink," he murmured, running his fingers over her outer lips. Then he delved into her core, and she jerked against his touch with a throaty moan. "And soaking wet, too."

"I-I can't help it, Daddy," she said. "I was thinking about what would happen when you came to my bedroom, and I started to get very achy between my thighs. I'm almost as unsettled as I was last night. Are-are you going to help me again?"

He swirled two fingers lightly over her clit.

Oh yes. Yes yes yes.

She arched into his expert caresses, and it didn't take long for her to reach the heights of pleasure. As a wave of ecstasy crashed over her, she shut her eyes and writhed against Daddy's roving fingers. After the last quaking pulse faded, she took a deep breath and opened her eyes, meeting his dark gaze.

Her heart skipped a beat.

Daddy was hovering over her, his lips mere inches from hers.

His hand remained between her thighs, but his fingers had ceased moving. Excitement rippled through her as he leaned down and pressed his mouth to hers.

It was a sweet, soft kiss, but it was everything to her.

When he finally pulled back, he stared down at her with affection brimming in his eyes.

"As long as you're a good little girl, Hanna, Daddy will visit you each night before bed to give you special rubs," he said. "Would you like that?"

She nodded wordlessly, her throat too closed up with emotion to speak.

Daddy had kissed her. A real kiss. A romantic kiss.

Oh, how she hoped he kissed her again.

Today and tomorrow and every day after that.

"Yes, Daddy," she finally replied. "I would like that."

"Good. So would I."

He withdrew a clean cloth from his pocket and used it to wipe the moisture from her inner thighs and then her privates, gently cleaning away the evidence of her arousal. Her face flamed with embarrassment over the intimacy of the act, but she didn't protest. She was starting to like when Daddy took care of her, and she also knew that if she protested too much, he might give her a scolding or even take her across his knee.

He reached for her panties and helped her back into them, then he pulled the covers over her and tucked her in. Before he departed the room, he kissed her again. She melted.

CHAPTER 12

Ben flipped through the mail as he walked back to the cabin with Lady bounding ahead after a squirrel. He watched the dog bark at the tree the squirrel ran up, and when he glanced down at the stack of bills and advertisements, he noticed a letter addressed to Hanna.

The air left his lungs. He stopped in the middle of the path to stare down at Eli's handwriting decorating the envelope. A few seconds passed before he recovered from the shock, and he shook his head to clear his thoughts.

Three weeks had passed since Hanna had come to stay with him, and even though she intended to see her brother again someday, the fact that she planned to eventually leave had been easily forgotten.

She filled his days and nights, bringing him more

happiness than he'd thought possible. Even though he hadn't taken her innocence, even though he hadn't taught her how to touch him sexually yet, they still shared a bond he despaired to break

Their connection went beyond anything sexual.

With the passing of each day, he longed to keep her forever at his side.

It was the height of selfishness though, because Hanna longed to leave. Or so she had claimed when she'd first arrived here.

Could her ambitions have changed? Dare he hope?

He clutched the mail and followed Lady, who was almost back at the cabin. It was ridiculous to believe Hanna would want to stay here. After all, the farm she'd grown up on was only a few miles away. The family who shunned her was surely in her thoughts, though she rarely spoke of them.

Ben paused at the bottom of the cabin steps, surveying his home and his land. He'd worked hard to build this fortress in the middle of nowhere. No one from his previous life could find him if they tried. He didn't have a landline and was therefore unlisted in the phone book. He had several burner phones he kept hidden in a closet for emergencies, but his name wasn't attached to them. And while he had a searchable address, Ben Foster was a pretty common name, and so far, none of his old friends, family, or acquaintances had contacted him by mail. Not that he thought they would be looking for him. Next month would mark his eighth year in these woods.

He glanced at the kitchen window and saw Hanna standing at the sink, oblivious to his presence. Could he leave the safety of his cabin for her? Would she withdraw from him if she knew of the reason he'd left his home in West Virginia? He sighed.

There was only one right thing to do at this moment.

He had to give her Eli's letter.

The smell of frying bacon reached him when he entered the cabin. He swallowed hard and headed to the kitchen, where he found Hanna placing two plates on the table. A beaming smile brightened her features when their eyes met. Her smile faded in an instant though, and she regarded him with genuine concern.

"What is it?" she asked. "Is something wrong?"

He forced a smile and held up Eli's letter. "No, nothing's wrong. This is for you."

She clapped her hands together and gasped in delight. "Finally. I was so worried he didn't get my last letter."

Ben passed her the envelope and wondered what Hanna had written in her last letter. A few days after she'd come to stay with him, she'd sent another letter off to her brother. Ben had shoved the sealed envelope into the mailbox, resisting the urge to tear it open in hopes of discovering her secret thoughts and dreams.

Anxiety twisted his stomach as Hanna ripped the letter open. She spread the folded paper out on the table and sat down, her eyes bright with curiosity.

Ben took a seat across from her, ignoring the breakfast she'd placed in his spot. "Did Annabel have the baby yet?" he asked, hoping Eli's wife had delivered their first child safely.

"No, not yet." Her eyes moved back and forth as she scanned the page. "At the time of this letter, Annabel is nine days away from her due date. Her doctor says baby and mother are both healthy. Eli says he's happy I left home and that he always knew I would. He wishes he could come see me right now, but he'll have to wait until the baby is born and they are settled back at home. He says his job is giving him two weeks off once the baby comes, and he will..." She paused and glanced up at Ben. Sadness replaced her prior joy, and she bowed her head to continue reading. She gulped and licked her lips before speaking. "He says once Annabel and the baby are settled at home, he'll come get me. He wants me to come to Oregon to live with them."

The emptiness inside Ben knew no bounds. He felt like he'd already lost the most important thing in his life, even as she stared at him from across the table. Sweet little Hanna. He did the math in his head, calculating exactly how many days he might have left with her. Even if Annabel had the baby today, he would have at least two weeks or more with her. Perhaps even longer, if Eli decided to drive instead of fly. Ben inquired if he'd indicated his method of travel in the letter, and Hanna said he had not.

"You don't look happy." He reached for her hand and laced his fingers through hers atop the table.

Tears pooled in her expressive blue depths, and she sighed and pushed the letter away with her free hand. "Of course I am happy," she said, smiling as a tear ran down her cheek. She brushed it away and tried to wrench her hand from his as she stood up. "Let me go, Daddy." Her voice trembled.

Daddy. She hadn't called him Mr. Foster in quite some time. The affection in her voice when she called him Daddy always filled up the empty places in his soul. She completed him each and every day, over and over again. She didn't balk when he called her his little girl. If anything, she craved it. He saw the need to be cared for in her eyes each time their gazes collided. The bond between them had grown more each day, alongside her growing trust in him.

But now she was leaving.

Their relationship was ending before it even had a chance to begin.

Hanna made another half-hearted attempt to yank her hand from his, but Ben still didn't release her. Instead, he pulled her closer and brought her down in his lap. He cradled her as she cried softly in his chest.

No words passed between them, but their hearts bled together as the sun danced through the window and spilled over her golden hair.

He kissed the top of her head, letting his lips linger as he breathed in her feminine scent. He should be happy to see Eli again after all these years. He should be happy to see Hanna reunited with her brother, and happy that Eli wanted to give her a safe place to stay, a family to be a part of.

But Ben wasn't happy at all. By God, he wasn't ready to let her go. He would never be ready to let her go. Three weeks. Three weeks was all it had taken to turn his world upside down.

And the pretty, innocent blonde in his lap had done so with her mere presence.

"Hanna," he said. "Little girl. Talk to Daddy. Tell me why you're crying."

She sniffled, and he used a napkin she'd set out for breakfast to dab her eyes and nose. She attempted to smile up at him through her tears, and his heart contracted to see her sweetness shining through her sorrow.

"I'm sorry," she said. "I didn't mean to cry."

"Shh. It's okay. You can cry anytime you'd like, but I'd like to know what has you so upset." He stroked her hair as he spoke in a gentle voice, trying to coax the truth from her.

"I want to see Eli again, and I want to meet his wife and baby, but Oregon is so far away." She peered at him with a vulnerable look. "It's so far away from you, Daddy."

He cupped her face in his hands and brought his lips to hers, kissing her hard until they both became breathless. "You can stay here with me for as long as you'd like, or you can go with Eli. The decision is yours, Hanna. Tell me what you want." He couldn't beg her to stay, not when she was in such a vulnerable state. Eli was the only family she had now, and it wouldn't be right for him to keep her away from her brother.

"I don't want to think about leaving you right now," she said, running a hand through his hair. "I just want... I want..." Her face reddened and she fumbled for words. But Ben felt her bottom pressing against his crotch, and she squirmed overtop him as his desire grew. She'd rubbed up against him a few times over clothing, but she'd yet to touch his cock, she'd yet to take it in her hand or... anywhere else.

"Tell me what you want," he said, his teeth clenched as he bit back a groan.

"I want you to take me to bed, Daddy. I want you to be inside me," she said. "Please, Daddy. Right now."

CHAPTER 13

THE MATTRESS DIPPED beneath Hanna as Daddy pressed her down on the bed. He hovered over her, trailing burning kisses along her neckline as she encouraged him by arching her center into his. Through his jeans, she felt his hugeness and knew it belonged inside her, deep in her feminine core.

She didn't want to leave the cabin.

Didn't want to leave Daddy.

And yet staying felt foolish.

Leaving Pennsylvania had always been her goal. Putting as many miles as possible between herself and the farm had always been her goal.

She hadn't counted on Eli coming to get her so fast. She'd thought she would have months. Months with Daddy. Months to find a better option, an option that gave her everything her heart desired—

experiencing life in the English world, spending time with Eli and his family, and of course, being with Daddy through all of this.

He'd spent years perfecting his little homestead here in the woods. The greenhouse and gardens. The storage rooms beneath the cabin. His existence whispered of dark secrets, but he'd yet to open up about the reasons for his separation from a previous life she could only speculate about.

His tongue entered her mouth and her worries floated away. She gyrated her hips against his, loving the feel of his stiff bulge rubbing against her achiness, soothing it, yet spurring it to pulse hotter. Urgency consumed her senses.

Hanna worked the buttons on his flannel shirt. The mornings had recently grown cooler, and today was the first day she'd seen him in anything but a t-shirt. It hugged his muscles and broad chest, and she gave him a small smile as she reached the last button and tugged the shirt from his jeans. He shrugged the garment off, as well as his undershirt, and tossed them away.

Then he pierced her with a dark look and pushed a hand up her dress, slipping a finger past her underwear to delve straight into her wetness.

"Oh!" she cried, whimpering low in her throat as he swirled around in her moisture.

"Do you like that?" he asked. "Do you like it when Daddy touches your pussy?"

His crass words riveted her. "Yes, Daddy."

"Say it. Say you like it when Daddy touches your pussy."

She panted as she tried to form the words. Words she would have never dared utter. Like pussy. It was what he sometimes called her moist center, the part of her that had awakened to his masterful touches.

A light slap stung the inside of her thigh. "Say. It."

She drew in a deep breath and met his eyes. "I-I like it when you touch my pussy, Daddy."

"Ask me to put my finger inside your pussy."

"Please... please put your finger inside my pussy." She tensed up, though she longed to feel the fullness of penetration in a place he'd never been, even with something as small as a finger.

He'd stroked her plenty of times. He'd taught her how to pleasure herself, and he visited her at bedtime every night to assist with her releases. The second night he'd visited her to give her *special rubs*, when he'd kissed her on the lips for the first time, she'd silently pledged her devotion to him. Now the thought of leaving him made her feel like she was breaking a sacred oath.

Thickness slid into her slick pussy, and she cried

out her pleasure at the new sensation. More thickness filled her, and she looked at Daddy in question. He gave her a slight, encouraging smile and kissed her forehead.

"You're doing great. I have three fingers inside you now. But not all the way inside. Your innocence is blocking my passage." He leaned down, bracing himself with one hand on the headboard. "But I'm going to use my cock to break through that, Hanna."

He pumped his fingers in and out while she fought for air. This was bliss. Pure and simple. His fingers were magic. His touch was fire. His kisses were love and passion. His heart was beating in sync with hers, or so she imagined.

Daddy broke away long enough to tug her panties down, past her knees and ankles. The feral gleam in his eyes as he tossed them to the floor gave her a dark thrill. The roughness of his touches as he worked her dress over her head spoke of his need. She didn't quite understand what he'd meant when he said her innocence was blocking his passage, but she felt safe in his hands. He knew what he was doing, and he seemed to be good at it. Her body screamed for more of his rough touches, more of his hard kisses and crass words.

"You're so beautiful, Hanna." He gazed at her and cupped her breasts.

She glanced down, past her heaving chest and at her complete nakedness. Peering back up at him, she smiled shyly and spread her legs in invitation. Daddy stood up to remove his pants. Her eyes didn't leave him as he stepped out of them, taking his underwear down too.

Her gaze landed on the stiffness between his legs, and her heart skipped a beat.

Daddy was huge.

Much too big for her.

Panic had her scrambling to crawl under the covers, but he pinned her down and positioned his hugeness between her thighs. Her pussy quaked, despite her fear over the pain she realized would come. His fingers had filled her up, and she feared a larger intrusion now that she'd seen how massive his manhood actually was.

"Hanna, look at me." Daddy's deep voice pulled her to him.

She met his gaze. The affection reflecting in his eyes chased some of her insecurities away.

"Spread your legs wider," he said. His tone was gentle, so kind. The rough touches and kisses had ended, but she enjoyed this side of him too, especially in this moment of uncertainty.

"Is it going to hurt?" she asked.

"Probably, but it'll be quick. I promise. Then I'll make you feel good, okay?"

She hesitated to answer and tried to turn her head, but he held her face firmly in his large, warm hands, stroking the side of her cheek with one finger. A smile turned his lips up briefly.

"Do you trust Daddy?" he asked.

Unable to form a single word, she nodded.

Of course she trusted him.

Her trust in him grew more each day, along with her desire to stay by his side always.

"It will only hurt this first time, Hanna."

"All right. Do it." She braced for the pain, shutting her eyes tight.

"Look at Daddy." He tapped the side of her face. "Eyes on me the whole time."

The moment their gazes met, he grabbed a square packet from the nightstand, ripped it open, and produced something thin and clear which he rolled over his shaft. The tip of his length teased her entrance, and then he surged forward.

His thickness filled her, burning as if she was being torn up from the inside. She winced and gasped at the same time but managed to keep her eyes open and on Daddy.

Despite the pain and her nervousness, she found looking at him helped to calm her nerves.

"Hanna, little girl, you're so tight." He groaned and withdrew slightly, only to surge forward again.

She tore her hands from the covers and circled her arms around his waist. His flesh heated under her touch, and she ran her hands up and down his back, soaking up the feel of his strong masculine body.

The burning pain lessened bit by bit as he moved within her depths.

In and out, and in and out.

He set a slow rhythm, and it wasn't long before the delicious achiness reignited.

She lifted her legs and squeezed his body, but he stiffened abruptly, and then his face tightened with a pained look.

"Does it hurt you too?" She hadn't considered this possibility.

He stilled mid-thrust. "No, Hanna. This doesn't hurt me at all. Quite the contrary."

"Then why do you look like you're about to pass out from pain?"

He inhaled deeply and began moving inside her again. The friction of his huge length stretching her as he thrust in and out drove her wild, and she wanted more. Faster. Harder. Her nails dug into his back, enough to draw a moan from him.

"I'm not about to pass out from pain," he finally answered, though his strange expression remained.

"I'm trying to go slow, so I don't hurt you, Hanna. It's your first time and I want to be gentle with you. It's taking every bit of my self-control not to pound into you hard and fast. You feel that good around my cock."

His words sank in, and she arched her center upward, meeting one of his thrusts. Surprise lit his features, but the pained look remained. She realized her movements had increased his pleasure, and she did it once more, only for him to stop and pin her down on the bed, holding her wrists in his hands.

"Young lady, I suggest you not do that. Not this first time."

"Why not?" She squirmed beneath him, trying to push him up.

"Because you're going to make me lose control."

Her smile faded and she regarded him thoughtfully. She leaned up and found his neck, and her lips danced across his flesh. The huge shaft buried within her pulsed, though he hadn't resumed his movements yet. Her lips parted and she dragged her teeth down the side of his neck. The already firm grip on her wrists tightened, and he drew back and gave her a look that bordered on anger. Hanna wasn't afraid though. She wanted him a little bit angry. Wanted him to lose control.

"Please, Daddy," she said. "I'm aching so much, and I want it hard and fast. Don't hold back."

A growl ripped through the air, and he soon released her wrists, only to grab her hips in a grip just as firm. His fingers dug into her flesh, and he hovered over her, panting and fierce.

"Don't forget you asked for this, little girl."

He withdrew his length before slamming into her, hard and deep. The air left her chest, and her pussy clenched around his shaft. His lower stomach hit her clit with each thrust. Her nipples tightened, and each brutal plunge brought her closer and closer to the release Daddy had shown her time and time before. Except this time, it wasn't due to his fingers or hers caressing her sensitive flesh. This time the orgasm built and built, past the point that she could bear it. She writhed against him, moving her hips in tune with his, trying to reach that blissful peak that would shatter her to pieces.

Sweat glistened over their bodies as they met thrust for thrust. He threw his head back and pounded her harder. Her heart swelled as she watched his movements, and his every little response to her touch. The sound of his groans when she dug her nails into his back swam in her head.

He leaned down to speak into her ear but maintained his fast pace of claiming her. "Tell Daddy to fuck you harder. Tell Daddy to fuck you harder and come inside your pussy."

Her vision blurred, and she spoke quickly, realizing she was about to reach that peak. "Fu... fuck me harder, Daddy, and... and come inside my pussy."

Jerky motions replaced his rapid, steady thrusts, and his whole body tensed.

Dark spots continued to dot Hanna's vision and she gave up watching him to close her eyes. She reached her peak and shattered, harder than she'd ever shattered before.

The pulsing between her legs stole her thoughts and drained her energy, leaving her weak but satisfied as she floated down from her high.

The world had faded long ago, and there was only Daddy.

CHAPTER 14

BEN RUBBED his eyes and reached for his coffee. He tried to concentrate on the work glaring from his computer screen, but his thoughts continuously strayed to Hanna.

A week had passed since the night he'd taken her innocence, and they'd spent every possible waking moment together since then. Even when he had work to do, she would sit in his office as she studied the G.E.D. prep books Eli had left behind.

He'd just placed his coffee down when her soft voice startled him.

"Why don't you have a phone?"

Ben swiveled around in his chair and looked at Hanna. She'd opened his office door a crack and had only poked her neck inside. Her nervous gaze flickered from his face and around the room. Guilt washed over him that she'd caught him working. He'd promised to spend the next few days with her, giving her his undivided attention. He'd just woken up early today to finish one last work project while she slept.

"I looked all over the house," she said, inching through the door with a small step. "I couldn't find a phone anywhere."

He sighed and ran a hand through his hair. "Why do you want a phone?"

"I... I was only curious about why you didn't have one. And I thought all English had phones in their houses." She paused for a second, opened her mouth as if to say something else, and then closed it. She backed up and vanished from the room, closing the door before Ben heard fast footsteps in the hallway.

He jumped to his feet and raced after her. He wasn't about to let her shut him out, not when their time together was limited, their future uncertain. Following the sound of her escape—a slamming front door—he hurried outside. He spotted her curled into a ball on the glider, blanketed in the early morning darkness. Lady was there too, sitting in front of Hanna, as if keeping guard. Ben approached and scratched Lady's ears before urging the dog back inside.

"Go on," he whispered.

The German Shepherd reluctantly obeyed, traipsing through the open door with her tail low.

"Hanna." Ben went to his sweet little girl, scooping her up to cradle her in his arms. She pushed at his chest and squirmed against his attentions.

"I want to know you," she said. "I want to know you and you won't speak of your past. I don't know anything about your family, your friends, or why you live out here alone. But even though I don't know you, I'm not ready to leave. Eli included his phone number in the letter, and I wanted to call him to tell him not to rush. To give me more time. To give *us* more time together. But how can I do that when you have so many secrets?"

Every muscle in his body tensed, and a chill moved through him. He grabbed her wrists, holding one in each hand to prevent her escape. Her eyes flamed wildly, and her face glimmered pale as a ghost in the lingering moonlight. The chorus of nighttime insects swelled around them, seemingly louder as the seconds ticked by and the tension between them escalated.

Ben had no choice. He had to tell her.

Had to toss his secrets at her feet and hope for the best.

He wasn't sure where or how to begin, but he started talking.

"I'm from a small town in West Virginia, Hanna. I lived there my whole childhood, went to college nearby, moved back and got married. I owned a computer repair shop with my wife, and the shop was located in the bottom of our house. One night I heard a crash and thought someone was breaking in to rob the business, so I grabbed my gun." His voice cracked, and his heart pounded fast as he watched Hanna's face grow whiter. "When I reached the top of the stairs, I thought I saw a man walking up, and when I told him to stop, he kept moving up the stairs, almost running. It was dark. I didn't turn on any lights and it was so fucking dark. The figure lifted his hand though, and I thought I saw him holding a weapon of some sort."

"What happened then?" She was no longer struggling to escape his lap, and she regarded him like a child watching the scariest part of a horror movie. Sympathy also shone in her eyes, as if she knew what Ben was about to confess to.

"I shot at him. The sixteen-year-old boy who lived next door. His name was Devon. The... the bullet only grazed his shoulder, but he fell backward down the steps and cracked his skull open. He died three days later. He didn't have a weapon on him, either, by the way. Just his cell phone."

Ben felt like he was outside of his body as he

described the following weeks to Hanna, which led to his exile in these woods. Devon had been the all-American boy—star of the football team, a straight-A student, leader of his youth group at church, and he'd already had a full scholarship to college.

After a lengthy investigation, authorities deduced that Devon had been returning from a party that night, and the boy had been so intoxicated that he'd entered the wrong house through a back door.

In the end, Ben was painted as the bad guy.

The community where he'd spent his whole life ostracized him. Even his wife, Carmen, no longer wanted anything to do with him. Reporters called day and night, and a few local news stations had a field day with the story.

After his divorce was finalized, Ben's only goal was to find a quiet, secluded place to live out the rest of his life. A place far away from accusing eyes. A place where no one would know a thing about him. A place where his past wouldn't haunt him. So, he'd moved to the backwoods of Pennsylvania.

"That's why I live out here alone. That's why I don't have a phone—at least not a landline like you were looking for. There's no one I need to talk to. I made a mistake. A terrible one. And not a day passes that I don't regret what I did. If I'd turned on a light first, if I'd waited for the boy to speak. If..." His voice trailed off.

Hanna remained frozen, holding his gaze with an expression he couldn't place. But it must be disgust. How else would she look at him? Her people abhorred violence and weapons.

He gently lifted her and placed her back on the glider. After one last stroke of her hair, which she didn't lean into the way she normally did, he stood up and headed for the front door. Pausing, he glanced back over his shoulder, feeling another chill creep up his back. "Now you know me, Hanna."

Lady scampered past him as he entered the house, no doubt going where she was needed most. Ben returned to his office and stared out the window. The outlines of the trees emerged after a short time, and the stars above faded one by one as the sky grew lighter. But just as the sun began to rise, a cloud cover moved in, ushering in a gentle rain. The patter of water on the roof lulled him into a miserable trance.

What had he been thinking? That he could send Hanna away with his good image intact? Her heart would've been broken whether he'd confessed his misdeeds or not. At least now she had a reason to avoid him. A reason to leave.

Perhaps her heart would heal sooner now that the cold, hard truth was out. The deep pangs of regret he'd felt in the moments and weeks after pulling the trigger vibrated in his chest, sharp and painful as he once again considered his actions.

He shouldn't have fired blindly into the darkness that night. He should've locked the bedroom door and called the cops. Maybe he should've fired a warning shot or called out one more time to Devon. The tragic incident had rocked his town and the surrounding communities. Ben wasn't charged with murder, though most of his town had called for it. No one, not even Carmen, had been able to forgive him. He liked to think his parents would've, but they'd died a few years before the incident.

The rain picked up, and Ben braced a hand on the window, watching the water drops run down the pane erratically. He'd been halfway sane before Hanna had come along. She'd shaken him with her sweet spirit, and he still felt possessive of her, and fiercely protective of her too. He still felt like she belonged to him, even though the rational part of his brain told him the possibility of keeping her was officially out of reach.

Perhaps the possibility of keeping her had always been out of reach and he'd been living in a fantasy world the past few weeks.

"Fuck," he muttered, backing away from the window.

He spun around and came face to face with Hanna. The office door was wide open, and she stood in the center of the room, watching him. He wondered how long she'd been standing there in silence.

His arms tingled with the need to wrap around her, to hold her tight and never let go. His gaze bored into her as he searched for any indication of her thoughts toward him. Her mesmerizing blues had a glassy look. Her lower lip quivered, and she bit it as if to quell her crying. Long, untamed blond locks streamed around her face, and she stood up straighter as they faced one another. The t-shirt and pajama pants she wore clung to her womanly form, hugging her body in all the right places. Her chest rose and fell rapidly, drawing attention to her full breasts and nipples that strained against her shirt.

"I don't understand," she said, reaching for his hand. Her gentle touch soothed his sorrow, if only a little.

"What don't you understand?" He thought he'd spelled it out clearly on the porch. He'd killed a man. A boy. He'd been violent in the worst way in her people's eyes.

"I don't understand why your town pushed you away. You confessed. You said you were sorry. And it was an accident. You didn't know it was a boy. You thought he was an intruder who meant to harm you."

"My town pushed me away because of what I did. It makes no difference to them whether I'm sorry."

Her brows knitted together, and she glanced at his chest. "I... I still don't understand."

Her reaction left Ben perplexed. "How would your people handle a murder?" he asked. "What if your father killed a neighbor, or one of your brothers? What would happen?"

She didn't blink at his question. "A period of shunning might occur, depending on the sin, but no one is pushed away permanently. Any crime, any sin, is forgiven if the sinner confesses to the bishops and asks for forgiveness."

"That's crazy."

Tears welled in her eyes. "Yes, I suppose it is." She reached for his face and caressed his cheek. "Eli told me our people sometimes cover up crimes in order to keep the English out of our affairs. He says he believes we are just as violent and sinful as the English though, and that's why he wasn't afraid to leave. He always told me not to fear the outside world. He said he would rather live in a world with few secrets than a world steeped in them."

Ben sighed. "He was pretty smart for a sixteen-year-old kid."

She smiled at him through her tears. Acceptance shone in her eyes, and her voice shook with emotion when she finally spoke. "I think it's time you bought a phone." She rose up on her toes to kiss his cheek. "Daddy."

A burning lump lodged in his throat, and he found himself blinking back tears of his own.

Daddy.

With a single word she'd given him more love and understanding than he'd felt in his whole life.

CHAPTER 15

Darkness surrounded Hanna, and the stars sparkled in all their heavenly brilliance above. She took a sip of steaming tea and leaned back in the glider, rocking it slowly with one toe pressed to the porch. The hot liquid rolled down her throat, spreading out from her center and warming her insides.

After the emotionally draining day she'd had, she needed this bit of respite. She also needed some thinking time before she called Eli. She planned to call him tomorrow afternoon using one of Daddy's burner phones and hoped her brother hadn't already left for Pennsylvania.

What would she tell Eli? And Daddy?

She had a decision to make.

One would take her far across the country to an unfamiliar place, but she would be with her brother.

The other would keep her close to Daddy, though only miles away from the childhood home she wished to forget.

Of course, she didn't want to forget *all of it*. She missed the children, her nieces and nephews, and little cousins. She even missed stubborn Sarah, as well as Abram and Jacob. She didn't miss her daat though. Or the suffocating house and the pressure to join the church.

She shivered and reached for the blanket she'd brought outside. The same fleece blanket Daddy had wrapped around her the night she'd learned all about desire. She draped it over her shoulders, careful not to spill the tea, and stared up at the beautiful night sky as if it held the answers to her problems.

She couldn't even think of Ben Foster as Ben Foster anymore. The thought of calling him Mr. Foster felt odd. She liked the way Daddy rolled off her tongue, warming her insides like the hot tea. When he called her *little girl*, or sometimes *baby girl*, she gushed with joy and felt complete.

In a few short weeks, he'd given her a glimpse of all she'd been missing out on. Affection. Companionship. Kindness. And today, honesty. The daily physical contact with another person breathed life into her. A simple hug or a kiss on the cheek from Daddy filled her spirits to bursting.

The door opened, jarring her from her thoughts. Light spilled into the night as Daddy exited the cabin. He joined her on the glider, draping an arm around her shoulders. She leaned into him, wishing she could have it all. Eli. Oregon. The world. Daddy.

She shut her eyes tight and inhaled Daddy's familiar masculine scent, taking comfort in the strength of his presence. He didn't speak, and neither did she. There was nothing to say. There was nothing to do. Except stare at the stars and listen to the sounds of the night.

Tomorrow was coming, and the next day, and the day after that too. Soon the day would come when Hanna would have to make the hardest decision of her life.

She wished with all her heart that she could snap her fingers and freeze time.

Oh, if only...

CHAPTER 16

"Rise and shine, sleepyhead." Ben pulled the sheets off Hanna, who was curled up on his side of the bed. She hadn't spent the night in her room since he'd made love to her the first time, and she'd also taken to sleeping in later and later.

She rubbed her eyes and peered up at him, her expression forming into a cute pout. "It's too early." She tried to yank the covers back up, but he stilled her with a quick swat to her bottom.

"It's not too early. It's almost eight. You used to wake up before six when you first came to stay with me, Hanna."

She rubbed her backside and continued pouting. "Yes, but we stayed up late last night. It's your fault I'm sleepy. You wore me out. Now go away and let me sleep."

He crossed his arms and arched an eyebrow. After the emotionally intense day they'd had yesterday, he'd planned a special day for Hanna. He wanted to take care of her completely, like she was his baby girl, and he suspected she would be receptive to this treatment. But first, he needed her out of bed.

"Young lady, that is no way to speak to your daddy. Now get up, or you'll be one sorry little girl."

She defiantly reached down and pulled the covers over her head. "No," she said, her voice muffled through the sheets. "Go away!"

He easily confiscated the covers, throwing them over the foot of the bed and out of her reach. She curled into a ball and returned her head to the pillow, closing her eyes and feigning sleep. He sat down on the edge of the bed and stroked her hair. A frustrated sigh floated up from her, and she opened her eyes to glare at him.

"We're going to try something different today, Hanna. Well, a little different."

"What do you mean?"

"I'm going to take care of you all day, and you're going to let me take care of you. You're going to be a good girl for Daddy and do everything I say without putting up a fuss."

A glimmer of confusion touched her gaze. "But

you already take care of me. You've been taking care of me for almost a month."

He cupped the side of her face in his hand. Desire spiraled through him at the innocence she still possessed.

"I'm going to care for you the way a daddy cares for his baby girl, Hanna. Help you get dressed, make your meals, give you a bath, read you stories. I know we don't have much time left before Eli comes, and I want you to put all that worry out of your mind today and let me do these things for you. Do you think you can do that?"

Her confusion faded and she blinked a few times. Blushing, she met his gaze. "Yes, Daddy, I can do that."

"Good girl." He patted her thigh. "Now first things first. Let's get these pajama shorts off."

She frowned and curled back into a ball. "Why?"

"I gave you several chances to get up this morning, and you were quite grumpy. You also had a smart mouth. Little girls don't get to tell their daddies to go away. It looks like you'll be eating breakfast on a sore bottom."

"Oh, Daddy, I'm sorry. Please don't spank me. I'll be good all day. *Promise.*" She peered at him, beseeching him with her big blue eyes to let her out of this punishment.

"Are you arguing with Daddy even more?" he asked, leaning down.

She huffed and sat up in bed, drawing her knees to her chest. He reached for her hand, giving it a firm squeeze.

"Baby girls get spanked when they're naughty, Hanna. Now come on. Over my knee." He sat back and patted his lap.

She huffed again, but slowly draped herself over his thighs. Her legs dangled, not quite reaching the floor, and she buried her face in the covers. He shifted her so that her bottom was high in the air, in perfect position for a good, quick spanking.

Goosebumps rose on her arms as he tugged her shorts down, pushing them to rest directly above her thighs. His cock swelled at the sight of her cute little bottom in lace-trimmed white panties. She was so sweet, so lovely. He rubbed her backside overtop her underwear.

"You were a very naughty girl this morning," he scolded, still rubbing. "When Daddy tells you it's time to get up, you need to listen and not be so grumpy, and you especially need to keep the attitude out of your voice. You never, ever get to yell at Daddy and tell him to go away, Hanna. Do you understand?"

Her breath hitched and she squirmed over his lap. "Yes, Daddy. But I really don't want a spanking."

"I'm the daddy and I decide what my baby girl needs," he said, cupping her left cheek firmly. "And right now, I think you need a good, hard spanking on your bare bottom."

"Oh, please, Daddy!" she begged. "Not on my bare bottom!" She squirmed as he tugged at the waistband of her panties, but he soon had them pushed down to rest atop her shorts.

"Settle down, Hanna."

She stilled, but her breathing had picked up. She pressed her thighs together and lay rigidly over his knee. He chuckled at the way she was trying to hide herself from him.

"No, no," he said. "You don't get to tense up like that. And you don't get to keep your thighs together either. Relax your bottom and spread your legs a bit."

To his surprise, she didn't budge and remained tense and unwilling. He leaned down and pushed her shorts and panties all the way to the floor, yet she still didn't move her thighs apart.

The naughty girl. She definitely needed a good spanking this morning, especially to get her in the right mindset to spend the day as his baby girl.

Ben repositioned her, forcing his knee between her legs and angling her bottom away from the bed, causing her thighs to fly open and her center to be on full display. She gasped, no doubt realizing that this position left her even more vulnerable.

"Daddy can see all of you now, Hanna. You can't close your legs, and your backside is high up on my knee. Your cheeks are spread wide too. Daddy can see the pinkness between your pussy lips, and your bottom hole too. I must say I like this position. Maybe I'll put you in this position for all your spankings."

She whimpered and struggled, but with her legs still dangling above the floor there wasn't much she could do. His strength overpowered hers, and he easily captured her hands at the small of her back and pinned them in place.

"Please don't spank me, Daddy! I'll be a good girl."

Her movements caused her lower stomach to rub over his groin, and his cock throbbed with need. He pushed his desires down and refocused on the naughty girl over his lap.

"Daddy's going to spank you now, Hanna, and I want you to be good and take your punishment. It's going to be a hard spanking, and I'm not going to stop until your bottom is good and red."

He brought his hand down before she could protest further.

CHAPTER 17

Daddy covered Hanna's backside with rapid swats, centering most of his attention on the lower curve of her cheeks. The pain of her spanking grew alongside her humiliation. She felt naughty and exposed with her thighs spread so wide. She flushed from head to toe when she recalled his earlier comment.

Daddy can see the pinkness between your pussy lips, and your bottom hole too.

"Please, Daddy! I'm sorry!" She couldn't stop herself from pleading. The sting of his hand raged across her bottom and upper thighs, and the swift blows brought tears to her eyes, making her feel truly punished and repentant.

"Next time I say it's time to wake up, are you going to yell and tell me to go away?" A smack accompanied each word he spoke, most of them to her poor thighs.

"No, I won't. I promise!"

"Good. Your spanking is almost over, Hanna."

She didn't want to feel one more spank, but she didn't dare argue. Daddy was in charge, and, if she were being honest, she wouldn't have it any other way. For the first time in her life, she liked being under someone's authority. She craved Daddy's dominance, as strongly as she craved his love. Tears slid from her eyes, burning down her face.

She dreaded the call to Eli this afternoon, and she wondered if Daddy had forgotten about it. Worry after worry sped through her mind as pain engulfed her bottom, and she began to sob over his lap. She'd known her life would change drastically when she left her family home, but she'd had no idea it would be this drastic of a change.

"Let it all out," Daddy said in a gentle voice. He landed one last swat to each of her cheeks before turning her over and sitting her upright on his lap.

Sorrow consumed Hanna. After Daddy's scolding and the first few smacks to her bottom, remorse had settled over, but that emotion didn't hold a candle to the intensity of her emotions now. She wept into his chest once he folded her into his loving embrace.

She wept for those she'd left behind. Stubborn Sarah, and Abram and Jacob too. Her little nieces and nephews. Her cousins who visited the farm to help out most days. She wept and wept and wept. Daddy didn't seem to mind, and he held her tight in the circle of his strong arms, stroking her hair as he whispered comforting words into her ear.

"I know you have a lot on your mind, Hanna," he said. "You tossed and turned all last night, and you talked in your sleep too. I know you're scared to talk to Eli, and I know you don't want to make any decisions yet about staying or leaving. So, I'm going to ask you to trust me. I have a plan and I think you're going to like it. I don't want you to become overwhelmed, so let me talk to Eli today. I'll explain everything to you after I speak with him, okay?"

She considered his proposal. She liked the sound of it, but she felt a tad guilty for pushing her first contact with Eli back. It was just a day though. Surely Daddy would let her call Eli tomorrow if she wished. She exhaled in relief and drew back to peer into Daddy's handsome visage. He reached for the tissues on the nightstand and brought one to her face. A little smile tugged at her lips as he dabbed her tears away and even instructed her to blow her nose.

"I'm so used to corresponding with Eli through letters that the thought of hearing his voice after all these years scares me a little," she admitted. "And what if he insists that I leave, no matter what I want?"

The warmth of his lips on her forehead stilled the last of her racing thoughts. "I promise you don't have to do anything you don't want to. Eli has a good head on his shoulders, and I'm sure he'll listen to you. Please don't worry, Hanna."

Another tear ran down her cheek, and he wiped it away and kissed her forehead again. She rested her head on his chest at his urging. She could cuddle with Daddy all day, every day. He hadn't shaved in two or three days, and she purposely lifted her head to feel the scratchiness of his stubble on her cheek. Slowly, she reached up to trace his features, spending the most time on the lower half of his face.

He chuckled. "What?"

"I... I..." She flushed and tried to think of a way to tell him about her tiny obsession with his facial hair. "Each time I was preparing to sneak off and visit you, I would lay awake in bed the night before wondering if you would be freshly shaven, or... or like this."

His gaze flickered over her, and his eyes quickly darkened with lust. It had taken Hanna a while to understand all of Daddy's looks, but she now knew desire when it stared her in the face. Her heart beat faster.

"Which do you prefer?" he asked.

"This." She brushed her fingertips along his rugged jawline. "Definitely this."

She swallowed hard and licked her lips when his face inclined to hers. Pressing his mouth to hers, he claimed her gently at first, tasting her as he held her head between his hands. She responded by meeting his tongue, thrust for thrust, but still allowed him to control the pace of the kiss.

When he eventually broke away, she was breathless and yearning for more.

The stinging of her bottom coalesced with the aching of her pussy, and everything below her waist throbbed and called out for attention.

Of course, her stomach chose that inopportune time to growl, loud enough to get Daddy's attention.

"Let's get you dressed and then I'll make you some breakfast." He helped her to stand and grabbed her hand, leading the way to her bedroom. She tried to move past him to select her own clothing out of the closet, but he stilled her by placing a hand on each shoulder. "What are you trying to do?" he asked.

"Get dressed."

"No. I'm going to dress you. Now go take off your shirt off while I pick something out." He turned to the closet and slid the door aside.

She opened her mouth to argue but shut it immediately. Her sore bottom was a powerful incentive to obey, so she pulled her shirt off and tossed it in the hamper. She stood awkwardly with her arms wrapped around her center. She'd lost her panties and pajama bottoms during the spanking, and she didn't have a stitch of clothing on at the moment. The sunlight streamed through the sheer curtains, heightening her vulnerability.

Daddy produced a pink knee-length dress he'd insisted she get the day they went shopping. It had short puffy sleeves and the skirt of the dress flared outward, revealing two white frilly layers of fabric underneath. It was beautiful and feminine, and Hanna had wanted to wear it before, but she'd put it back in the closet each time she'd almost worn it to change into something plainer. Some habits were harder to break than others, but today Daddy wasn't giving her a choice.

He laid the dress on the bed and crooked a finger at her. "Come here, baby girl."

CHAPTER 18

BEN WATCHED as Hanna approached him. She'd dropped her arms from her waist and clasped her hands low in front of herself, as if trying to hide her privates. Her face was flushed prettily, and she bowed her head as she came to stand before him.

Her sweet submissive display, coupled with her shame over her nudity, called up his darkest, most depraved desires.

The things he wanted to do to her.

The things he wanted to teach her.

His cock swelled up and pressed painfully against his jeans.

"Turn around so Daddy can see how well-spanked your bottom is."

Her eyes widened at his request. Hesitance flashed over her face, and she bit her lower lip. She unclasped her hands and reached back, rubbing her bottom. "It's very well-spanked, Daddy. Trust me. It still hurts."

He smirked. "I'm sure it does, but I want you to turn around and show me."

A soft sigh escaped her, and her shoulders hunched in defeat as she obeyed. His cock twitched and his balls tensed up at the sight she presented. He guided her a few steps to the right and urged her to bend over the bed. He stroked her rosy cheeks.

"Your bottom still feels hot, Hanna. And it's bright red, too."

She whimpered, and he wasn't sure if it was out of embarrassment, pain, arousal, or a mixture of all three.

"Now remember, for the rest of the day, Daddy is in charge. You need to be a good baby girl, or I'll add more red to this bottom. Do you want to end up over Daddy's knee again?"

"No, Daddy."

"Then what are you going to do today?"

"Be a good girl." Her response came out in a shuddering whisper.

"That's right. Now you can stand up." He backed away and searched through the nearby dresser, choosing a pair of plain white cotton panties. When he faced Hanna, she had resumed her submissive pose with her hands clasped and her head bowed.

"Step into these." He bent slightly and allowed her to step into the panties, one leg at a time. She wobbled when she lifted one foot and placed her hands on his shoulders for balance. Ben pulled her panties up and paused as he reached for the dress. He'd expected her to be somewhat embarrassed as he dressed her, but the level of anxiety in her eyes was a bit over the top. Her feet shuffled in place, and she kept glancing at the bathroom door.

Of course. He should've asked if she had to pee before getting her dressed in the first place.

"Do you have to go potty, Hanna?"

Crimson bloomed on her cheeks, and she avoided his gaze.

"Answer me, young lady."

She whimpered and stared at her feet. "Yes."

"Come on, I'll take you potty." When she didn't follow immediately, he held out his hand.

"Can't I go by myself? Please, Daddy?"

"No. Now let's go before you pee your panties. If you have an accident, I'll have to put a diaper on you today."

Her little hand landed in his and she followed obediently. In the bathroom, Ben instructed her to wait next to the toilet while he slid her panties down to her ankles.

He hovered over her, taking in the sight of her flushed face and pretty, wide eyes. A surge of protectiveness tightened his chest, and he once again despaired at the thought of losing her. He hoped she liked his proposal regarding Eli, but he would save it for later when it was time for the big surprise. The evening couldn't come soon enough, but he shoved his anticipation down and focused on sweet little Hanna.

"Are you going to leave the bathroom?" she asked, biting her lip.

He shook his head and lifted her up, sitting her down on the toilet. She covered her face with her hands and sat as still as a statue.

"Please leave." She peeked at him through a few spread fingers.

"I'm not leaving. Now *go*. Do you want to wear a bulky diaper instead?"

That did the trick. She buried her face deeper in her hands and bowed her head as she peed.

"Good girl," Ben said once she'd finished. He lifted her off the potty and cleaned her up. She didn't uncover her face the whole time. "Are you going to hide from Daddy all day?"

Face still covered, she nodded stubbornly.

"Why?"

"Be-because I'm ashamed."

After quickly washing his hands, he pried her hands away from her face and lifted her chin up, forcing her gaze to his. "You have nothing to be ashamed about, Hanna. Daddy likes taking care of you. Now come on. Let's get these panties back up and get you dressed."

She tried to smile through her embarrassment, and her sweet attempt stole his heart a thousand times over. After he got her dressed, he brushed out her hair and led her to the kitchen where he prepared oatmeal and toast. He tucked a napkin into the front of her dress and watched her eat. She picked at her food, and it took a few stern looks to get her to finish.

"Daddy, may I please have coffee?"

"Sorry, baby, but little girls can't have coffee." He smirked, knowing she was testing him. He'd never seen her drink coffee before.

She huffed and tried to leave the table, but he leaned forward and caught her hand. "Finish your milk, young lady."

"But I am finished. I just don't want the rest of my milk."

He arched an eyebrow and sat back, crossing his arms over his chest. "Are you trying to test me,

Hanna? I suggest you be a good girl and finish your milk, unless you want to face the consequences."

Lady barked outside, and Hanna gazed longingly out the window. She still hadn't touched her glass.

"How about this? Finish your milk and then we'll go on a walk with Lady."

She lit up and nodded eagerly. Sunlight streamed through the windows, reflecting off her shiny golden hair as she reached for her cup. The last of her milk disappeared in seconds. He dabbed her face with a napkin, prompting her cheeks to redden once more.

"I have a feeling you'll be blushing a lot today, baby girl."

CHAPTER 19

Hanna rubbed her eyes and yawned. She rolled over, glancing at the clock on the nightstand and gasped. She'd napped for two hours in the middle of the afternoon! Smiling guiltily to herself, she recalled how she'd argued with Daddy that she wasn't sleepy. The walk through the woods with Lady must've tired her out more than she'd thought. She stretched and sighed as her bare legs caught the cool spots under the sheets.

A breeze blew through the window, the curtains dancing to the tune of the wind chimes. Sadness squeezed her heart. If she left with Eli, she would never wake up to the sound of those wind chimes again. Of course, it wasn't the actual loss of the wind chimes that darkened her spirits.

Daddy.

She'd grown to love him so much she couldn't breathe when she imagined a future without him.

Was it wrong and foolish to give up her dreams of moving so far away from the farm?

As far away as Eli had moved?

She wiped her tears and wondered about the conversation Daddy had had with Eli while she'd napped. Surely, he'd called her brother then, when she wouldn't have been able to overhear.

Whatever plan Daddy had, she hoped he realized how much she cared for him.

She resolved to work up the courage to tell him today.

It had to be today.

She loved him with everything inside her.

The secrets of his past didn't affect her love either. It had been an unfortunate accident, and she grieved to know he'd been hurt and alone for so many years. She grieved to know others hadn't treated him with kindness and offered him the forgiveness he'd desperately needed. The scorn and blame of his hometown had driven him to the remote mountains of Pennsylvania, and while she was glad he lived here, she wished his reasons for moving here weren't so dark.

The door opened and she sat up in bed, pushing the covers down.

"Hi, Daddy!" She smiled at him and laced her arms around his neck as he sat beside her. She placed a kiss on his cheek and hugged him tight.

"Did you sleep well?" The strength of his arms surrounding her made her feel safe and loved. While some of the things he'd done for her today had embarrassed her, like helping her in the bathroom and cleaning her face off after meals, a part of her liked being taken care of so thoughtfully. He made her feel treasured, and that was an emotion she wasn't used to experiencing.

"Yes, Daddy, I can't believe I slept so long."

He kissed the top of her head and drew back to gaze down at her. His expression turned serious, and her tummy fluttered. "Do you remember the plan I told you I had? The surprise?"

Her throat burned, and the uncertainty of not knowing became too much. She tried to answer, but her voice cracked, so she simply nodded.

"The surprise is outside. It arrived earlier than I expected. I think you'll like it. Let's get you out of your pajamas and back into that cute little dress, and we'll go outside together."

This time, Hanna wasn't shy about letting Daddy dress her. He laughed at her enthusiasm and grabbed her hand, leading her through the house to the front door. Lady was barking up a storm on the porch, and

Hanna wondered if they had a visitor. She regarded Daddy with curiosity, but he didn't give away any clues. If anything, he appeared nervous.

He dropped her hand and held the door open, nodding for her to step outside. Even though she trusted Daddy that it was safe, his excitement was contagious, and she peeked her head out the door first.

Lady shot down the steps, still barking. Hanna's gaze followed the dog through the overcast afternoon and landed on a huge bus parked in the grassy clearing in front of the cabin. No, not a bus. An RV.

Excitement raced through her, and she wondered if Eli had come, but as she left the porch and approached the RV, no one exited it. Daddy's footsteps sounded behind her as she peered into the windows. Nothing. No one. Eli hadn't come. He wouldn't have been able to drive this far in a day or two anyway. She felt silly for her error.

"Daddy..." Confusion settled on her and she spun to gaze at Daddy.

"It's an RV, Hanna."

She laughed. "I know what it is. Why is it parked here?"

"I bought it. It's the nicest one they had at the dealership in town. They delivered it while you were napping."

She looked from Daddy to the RV. If he'd bought this huge, expensive thing, then he'd bought it for a good reason. To drive somewhere. To drive a long way in comfort. Maybe as far as Oregon. Her head snapped in his direction, and his guilty smile brightened the overcast day. But her spirits sank in the next moment.

What would happen between them once they reached Oregon, assuming that was indeed his plan?

He strode to her and clasped one of her shaking hands in his and brought it up to cover his heart. The pain in his gaze carried so much raw emotion she couldn't tear her eyes from his.

"Hanna," he began. He took a long breath before continuing. "I care about you very much. I don't want to stand in your way though, and I know you want to see Eli and visit his family."

"Daddy..."

"Let me finish." He stroked a hand down the back of her head, and she melted under his gentle touch. "I told you I had a plan. Well, here it is. We'll drive all the way to Oregon together, and we can take Lady with us in the RV too. We'll take the long way there so you can see whatever parts of the country you've been wanting to see. You can help me map out our trip. We'll visit Eli for as long as you'd like. We'll also..."

Hanna listened as Daddy went on and on about his plan. She thought it was brilliant. He confessed Eli wasn't thrilled about their relationship, but Daddy was certain her brother would come around eventually. They would stay with Eli's family for as long as Hanna wished, and Daddy said they could go anywhere in the continental United States in the RV. He could bring his laptop and continue to work on his website design business, and if Hanna never wished to set foot in Pennsylvania again, he would find a way to make it work. In short, they would still be together in the coming days.

Together indefinitely.

"I don't want to lose you, Hanna. I love you very much, and I'd like to be with you and take care of you for as long as you'll let me."

Daddy's profession of love burned into her memory. For as long as she lived, she would never forget the moment he'd said he loved her. Not only was he the first person to ever speak of love to her, but he was the first man to teach her about love. He would always have her gratitude for that, no matter what happened in the years to come.

Joy filled her to overflowing. Grinning wide, she rose on her tiptoes and kissed Daddy on the lips. "I love you too, and I love your plan. This was the best surprise I can think of." She kissed him again. "Thank you, Daddy."

Relief spread across his face, and his shoulders relaxed. He squeezed her hand. "Come on, sweet girl. I'll show you the inside."

CHAPTER 20

"Hanna!" Ben called. "Time for your bath!" He strode into the living room where he'd left her while he ran the water. She wasn't on the floor in front of the TV watching cartoons anymore, and he glanced around as he wondered if she was playing a trick on him.

His palm twitched as he also wondered if she was up to something naughty. He suspected she was hiding behind the curtains or the couch.

"Hanna, baby girl, you'd better come out by the time I count to three! One. Two. Three."

Hanna didn't appear, but a noise in the kitchen caught his attention. Slowly, he crept through the house in the direction of the noise. He peered through the doorway and caught sight of his baby girl pushing a chair up to the refrigerator. Drawing back into the shadows of the hallway, he continued to spy.

She bit her lip and glanced around, as if making sure he wasn't nearby. The guilty look on her face was so adorable he almost laughed. She crawled up on the chair and reached for the cookie jar he'd placed there earlier. He'd told her if she was a good girl, he would let her have a cookie after dinner tonight. The naughty, naughty little girl was trying to sneak behind his back and steal a cookie while he ran her bath.

Without speaking, he entered the kitchen, picked her up by the waist, and set her down on the floor. The shock on her face as she gawked up at him was priceless.

"Da-Daddy. I was just... I was..." She bowed her head and shuffled her feet.

"I know very well what you were doing," he said, crossing his arms. "You were being naughty, Hanna."

"Yes, Daddy," she admitted. "I'm sorry."

"You know very well that the cookies were for after dinner. I'm very disappointed that you got up to mischief while I was preparing your bath, baby girl."

"I won't do it again," she said, her eyes pleading.

"I'm glad to hear that, Hanna, but I think a red bottom will help remind you to behave in the future."

He dragged the chair away from the refrigerator and into the center of the kitchen.

"Please don't spank me, Daddy! My bottom is still sore from this morning."

"Not sore enough, apparently." He smirked as he sat down and patted his thigh. "Come on. Over my knee, baby girl. Let's get your spanking over with quickly so your bathwater doesn't go cold."

Her hands flew behind her and she cupped her bottom.

"Hanna," he warned. "One. Two..."

She hurried to his side before he made it to three. "Please not hard, Daddy."

Locks of golden hair obscured her face as she tucked her chin down, staring at the floor with a trembling lower lip. He hated to cause her tears, but he suspected she'd been testing him by leaving the living room. To go soft on her now would be a mistake. He needed to be firm in his discipline, lest she try to get away with naughtier schemes in the future.

He guided her across his lap and rubbed her bottom over her dress. "Good baby girls don't try to sneak cookies before dinner, and good baby girls most certainly do not stand on chairs. You could have fallen and hurt yourself."

"But..."

He swatted her backside twice. "Quiet, Hanna. You know you were naughty, and you know you deserve this spanking, don't you?"

A defeated sigh left her, and her shoulders slumped. "Yes, Daddy."

Ben decided he'd scolded her enough, so he set into her bottom, spanking her with hard swats over her dress. As he spanked, he peeled back the layers of her skirt, slapping her backside a few times before lifting another layer and giving her more punishment. Redness showed through the last layer of the white fabric, and he flipped it up to reveal her panty-clad bottom.

"Such a naughty baby girl." He yanked her panties down to her knees.

"Please, Daddy," she said, squirming. "Please, that's enough spanking."

"I decide when you have enough." With that, he laid into her reddened butt with rapid smacks. She kicked her feet and reached back to cup her bottom. Clucking his tongue, Ben gathered her wrists in one hand and secured them at her lower back.

Sobs broke through as her struggles ceased. Her shoulders heaved and her legs stopped kicking. Ben placed a dozen blows to her lower bottom to drive the lesson home before stopping to caress her glowing mounds. A string of apologies flew out of her mouth as she cried, and he lifted her and turned her to sit in his lap, the urge to comfort his baby girl overwhelming. Her panties had fallen to the floor, and her heated bare bottom rested on his thighs.

"It's all right now, baby girl," he soothed. "Your spanking is over, and all is forgiven, all right?"

She sniffled and nodded. "All right. Sorry again, Daddy."

He cupped her face and kissed her forehead. "I know you are. Now, come on. It's bath time."

Ben led her to the master bathroom. He wiped the last of her tears away with a tissue and dabbed her nose. Adoration shone in her eyes as she gazed up at him, and he gave her another hug before tugging her dress over her head.

CHAPTER 21

HANNA RUBBED her sore bottom as Daddy tested the bathwater.

She never should have left the living room, but she'd been on her way to ask Daddy if she could have just one little cookie before dinner when she'd decided to sneak one instead. She'd thought she would have enough time before he came back.

Of course, the thrill of possibly getting caught had played a part in her naughtiness too.

She cupped her burning backside and winced.

Getting caught hurt.

"Do you have to go potty, baby girl?" he asked.

Though he'd taken her to the bathroom a few times today, and a part of her liked being taken care of that way, it still embarrassed her thoroughly. She covered her face and nodded. Daddy picked her up and sat her on the toilet, and she kept her face hidden as she peed.

"Next time we do a baby girl day, Hanna, I'm going to put you in diapers."

She uncovered her face and stared at him in shock. Her pulse accelerated and her insides fluttered, and her face grew so hot that her ears and neck burned too.

"I have never seen you blush so hard, Hanna." He lifted her off the potty and cleaned her, then helped her into the bathtub.

Hanna sank down in the bubbles, gasping as her tender backside hit the warm water. She was grateful to be able to hide underneath the soapy water and tried not to think about the shame she would endure during the next baby girl day, though thinking about it caused heat to surge between her legs.

All the muscles in her body relaxed as Daddy scrubbed her gently with a washcloth. She sat up in the water when he instructed and lifted her arms and even gave him her feet to scrub. He was very thorough and methodical as he washed her all over.

"All right, baby girl, stand up so Daddy can clean your bottom now."

"My bottom is clean. I've been sitting in hot soapy water." She was still reeling from his promise to put her in diapers, and now he intended to shame her further. It probably wasn't smart to argue, but she couldn't help it. "Please, Daddy, I'd just like to get out of the tub."

"Stand up." One thick eyebrow arched up, and the lines on his forehead creased. He looked especially stern.

Water cascaded down her body as she rose up, sighing in frustration as she did so. Daddy immediately began soaping her up between her thighs, and she whimpered at his touch. She whimpered even louder when he slipped a finger into her bottom hole as he washed her.

"Next time we have a baby girl day, you'll be in a bulky diaper and a short dress all day long," he said as his finger moved in and out of her bottom hole. "You'll have to lie down on the floor so Daddy can change you after you wet yourself. And if I catch you trying to use the potty like a big girl, guess what will happen?"

"I... I'll get a spanking?" Her voice wavered and she struggled to remain standing.

"That's right. You'll get a spanking. I'll take your diaper off and paddle you with a hairbrush for being such a naughty baby girl, Hanna." As he spoke, his fingers worked magic behind the washcloth, smoothing over her throbbing center as he described her future humiliation.

Hanna's chest rose and fell rapidly. There wasn't enough air in the room, and she needed more of Daddy's touch. Her nipples tightened painfully and her breasts ached something fierce. Her pussy felt slick, and not just from the soap. Desire spiraled outward from her core, and her achiness built as she began moving against Daddy's hand. The washcloth fell in the water, and his fingers replaced it, much to her relief. She rested one hand on his shoulder and the other against the wall to keep balance.

"Does that feel good?"

"Yes, Daddy."

One thick finger still penetrated her bottom hole, and he kept pumping it as he swirled another finger over her pulsing clit. Her legs felt as if they would give out at any moment, but she knew Daddy would catch her if they did.

The friction built and built, and he pressed a second finger into her bottom hole.

"Let go, baby girl. Daddy has you."

She let go, and when her legs gave out as the wave of pleasure consumed her, Daddy caught her in his arms.

CHAPTER 22

Ben gazed at Hanna from across the table. The pitter-patter of a light rain sounded on the roof. Lady was sprawled out in the middle of the floor, snoring and occasionally yipping and moving her legs as if chasing the squirrel that had eluded her yesterday. The lights were dimmed, and a single candle burned in the center of the table. Thunder boomed in the distance, and Hanna jumped in her seat.

"Are you scared of thunder?" he asked.

She shrugged and avoided his gaze.

"Hanna," he warned.

"Yes!" she whispered quickly, still refusing to meet his stare.

His protective instincts rose to the surface. "Are you finished with your spaghetti?" he asked.

She nodded, jumping in her seat as another crack

of thunder rang out. He cleared the table and threw the dishes in the dishwasher in record speed, then led Hanna into the living room. A single lamp illuminated the area dimly. He sank down on the couch and patted his thigh.

"Come sit on Daddy's lap."

She crawled onto his thighs, and he covered her with a blanket, wrapping her tight in his arms at the same time. She fit perfectly and nestled her head next to his heart. He decided now was as good a time as any to discuss their plans for the coming weeks, and he hoped talking would offer a distraction from the storm.

"It'll take a day or two to close the cabin up. When would you like to leave for Oregon?"

Instead of stiffening in his arms the way she normally did when the topic of leaving came up, she sighed and snuggled deeper into the blanket and his embrace. "Let's wait until Eli calls to say Annabel had the baby. Then by the time we arrive at their home, they'll have had some time alone to get used to their new family member. I know Annabel has lots of sisters and other family members nearby, so it's not like they'll need our help. What do you think?"

"Sounds perfect." Ben was nervous about driving off and leaving the cabin for an extended period for the first time in years. He would be out in the real world, but at least they wouldn't be traveling near his hometown and the pain of his past. He imagined Hanna gawking out the window of the RV as they drove through a city, or past a landscape unlike anything she'd seen before. The desire to show her the very things he'd spent years hiding from gave him the courage to take the bold step of leaving.

He would do anything for her, anything for his sweet baby girl.

"Daddy?"

"Yes?"

"I looked at the calendar today. Tomorrow's my nineteenth birthday."

Being reminded of her age no longer shocked him, but he was a little upset with himself that he hadn't asked when her birthday was. He'd known it was coming up soon. No matter. He would find a way to make it special. He tilted her chin up and let his stern gaze fall on her. His groin tightened at her light gasp and sudden nervous look.

"We have a tradition in the English world you may not be familiar with, baby girl."

"What tradition?"

"Birthday spankings."

She drew back in surprise. "Birthday spankings? I think you're making that up, Daddy!"

He lost control of his faux sternness and broke

into a smile. "Nope, I'm not making it up. It's true. You'll get twenty spanks in all tomorrow. Nineteen for your age plus one to grow on. Over my knee on your bare bottom, of course. It's the proper way for a daddy to give his little girl a birthday spanking."

Warmth hit his neck as her breathing increased. She squirmed on his lap, no doubt feeling his stiffness beneath her backside. But a second later, thunder rumbled overhead, closer than before, and it shook the cabin slightly. She stopped squirming and burrowed under the blanket, wrapping her arms tight around his waist.

He decided to distract her again and ducked under the cover to purposely graze her cheek with his stubble on his way to kissing her neck. She released her hold on the blanket and it fell away. The sharp peaks of her stiff nipples drew his gaze, and he leaned down to tease them through the thin fabric of her dress. He was glad he hadn't allowed her to wear a bra today because her response was immediate, her quick intake of air coupled with her chest thrusting upwards to receive his touch. Pulling back, he cupped her breast with one hand while his other hand traveled up her dress and past the barrier of her panties.

"My baby girl is soaking wet." He claimed her mouth then, and her tongue danced with his, gliding past his lips and within. He groaned and felt her rubbing his cock over his jeans. She'd slipped a hand underneath herself to squeeze and massage him, and his stiffness ached to be freed from its confines. He swirled a finger in her moisture before pushing inside her wetness, and her pussy clamped down on his digit. She no longer had her virginity, but she was still so deliciously tight.

He broke away to catch his breath and stared down at her. She glanced up, and the moment their gazes collided, thunder roared and lightning flashed, but she didn't jump in fear. Perhaps she hadn't heard the loud noise. He couldn't be sure why, but as the thunder crackled overhead again, she began tugging at his t-shirt, the storm outside apparently forgotten. Grasping her hands, he shook his head.

"No, no," he said. "Let's get that cute dress off you first."

Despite her eagerness, a blush stained her cheeks. He knew from prior experience with Hanna that it shamed her more to be unclothed while he was fully dressed. Yes, he was a bastard for enjoying her embarrassment, but he also wanted to keep the proper balance of power. In this relationship, he made the rules with her best interests at heart, and she followed them because he'd earned her trust. He was the daddy, and she was the sweet, sometimes naughty, baby girl. And when she was naughty, he was more than happy and willing to put her in her place.

He instructed her to stand and lift her arms up, and her face reddened more once he pulled the dress over her head and tossed it aside.

"Hands at your sides now," he said sternly.

She complied, remaining in place with her head bowed, wearing nothing but a pair of white cotton panties. Ben circled her a few times, touching and exploring her body in the process. He pinched a nipple, brushed her hair over her shoulder, stroked her ass, and watched with dark amusement as goosebumps covered her arms. He stopped behind her and yanked her hair back, just hard enough to make her gasp and whimper. His lips brushed her ear.

"You're going to take those panties off and get down on your hands and knees on the floor. Then you're going to arch your bottom up and take your Daddy's cock from behind like an obedient little girl."

Her breathless reply sounded like, "Yes, Daddy," but she spoke so fast he couldn't be sure. He released her hair, and she slipped her panties off and hit the floor, arranging herself on her hands and knees. The arching her bottom part gave her pause, and she took a few deep breaths before pressing her head to the carpet and lifting her ass high, presenting it to him like a good girl, just as he'd commanded.

The sight of her enticing sweetness, so moist and pink, and her bottom which still bore redness from her recent spankings, ignited his libido full force.

He stripped his clothing off and knelt behind her on the floor with his cock in hand.

"I'm going to pound you long and hard, Hanna, and you're going to take every thrust I give you like a good little girl."

CHAPTER 23

Daddy's lewd words never ceased to thrill Hanna. Moisture dripped from her core to the inside of her thighs, evidence of her need to be taken just as he'd described.

She heard the tear of foil. A condom. He'd explained to her what the square packets were for, and a few times she'd assisted in covering his massive length with the thin, clear safeguard.

Her pussy convulsed when he placed the tip of his sheathed cock at her entrance, pulsing in anticipation of his thickness ramming into her. She whimpered as he traced his length around her slick folds, tormenting her throbbing parts as she tried her best to force his touch to her hardened nub. Of course, he came close a few times, but seemed to purposefully avoid it, so she balanced herself on one hand and reached underneath her stomach to stroke it herself.

Thwack! No sooner had she reached her destination than he'd slapped her bottom. Hard. The sting amplified the achiness between her thighs, but she placed her hand back on the floor, hoping Daddy would enter her soon. She felt ready to burn up, and perspiration trickled down her temple.

"Sorry, Daddy," she murmured, feeling deeply repentant.

"That better not happen again. I'll decide when and if you come tonight, Hanna. Touch yourself again and I'll spread your thighs wide and spank your privates."

Disbelief jolted through her, and she wondered if he meant it. She decided not to test him and kept her hands flat on the floor, her hips raised with her pussy on display for his taking.

If only he would take it.

The yearning to be filled had her heart pounding harder by the second. Her breasts hung heavily beneath her, and her nipples were so hard and tingly it felt as if they'd ignited.

The waiting was agony.

"Please, Daddy," she begged. "*Please please please.*"

Again, he traced her slick nether folds with his

cock, spreading her wetness all around, everywhere but her bereft clit. "I like it when you beg," he said, his voice deep and husky. "Beg some more. I want to hear you say the naughty things you'd like Daddy to do to you."

She hesitated. He'd often instructed her to repeat crass phrases after him, word for word. But to come up with such words on her own? To honestly speak her desires aloud?

Her face heated, and more perspiration rolled down her temples.

She would combust if he didn't take her now.

She closed her eyes, feeling her shame soar higher with her imminent confession.

"Please, Daddy," she said. "I want you to fuck my pussy hard. And touch my clit so I can... so I can come. I can't bear to be here on the floor for one more moment without you inside me."

He grasped her hips and surged forward, filling her up completely with one hard thrust. All the air left her lungs in a rapid whoosh, and the room spun and spun.

Somehow, she managed to hold position on her hands and knees as he withdrew slightly only to shove back inside her swollen tightness.

Again and again.

He kept a firm hold on her hips and set a brutal,

possessive pace, making her feel like she belonged to him in every possible way.

Her mind. Her body. Her heart. Her soul.

All of it, his for the taking.

Her thoughts whirled with the ecstasy that consumed her, and she arched her center higher to meet his harsh movements as desire coiled in her lower stomach. Daddy pressing his finger to her clit was all it took to send her flying into oblivion. Her release cascaded outwards from her center, pulsing and rushing through her with a fury that had her panting and clawing at the carpet. Her heart pounded in her ears, and she cried out as Daddy's cock jerked within her depths and he joined in her release.

The heat from his chest radiated on her back. He was hovering over her, trying to catch his breath as she endeavored to catch hers. He recovered before she did and scooped her up in his arms and carried her to his bedroom.

The storm raged outside, lightning flashing through the curtains, but her fear didn't resurface. She felt safe with Daddy. He flicked on a lamp and disappeared into the bathroom briefly. When he returned, he spooned her on the bed as they watched the storm together. Eventually, it quieted down, the flashes ceasing as the thunder dulled to a faint, distant rumble. Even the rain stopped drumming on the roof.

Daddy broke the silence.

"Are you nervous?" he asked.

"About what?"

"The birthday spanking you have coming tomorrow."

She giggled. "Oh, that. Actually, I'm a little... um... excited about it. Is that strange?"

His warm hand cupped her bottom, squeezing as he kissed the back of her neck. "It's not strange. It's naughty. So very very naughty, young lady. I should take you over my knee right now, baby girl."

Desire stirred in her inner core, and she wiggled her bottom against his hand. "I can't help it, Daddy. I like being naughty for you." She turned over just in time to catch his unguarded response and laughed at the shock on his face.

Her heart swam with joy as she leaned in to kiss the man who'd taught her all about love.

ABOUT SUE LYNDON

USA TODAY BESTSELLING AUTHOR SUE LYNDON writes naughty, heartfelt romance filled with sexy discipline, breathless surrender, and scorching hot passion. Hard alpha males, strict husbands, fierce alien warriors, and stern daddy-doms make her go weak in the knees. She's a #1 Amazon bestseller in multiple categories, including Sci-Fi Romance, Historical Romance, BDSM Erotica, and Fantasy Romance. She also writes vanilla sci-fi romance under the name Sue Mercury —but no matter the genre or pen name, her books always have a swoon-worthy happily ever after.

WWW.SUELYNDON.COM

****Get FREE reads when you sign up for Sue's newsletter—and be the first to hear about freebies, sales, and new releases:**

https://www.suelyndon.com/newsletter-sign-up **

www.ingramcontent.com/pod-product-compliance
Lightning Source LLC
Chambersburg PA
CBHW071942150726
47999CB00001B/294